# TWO SPINSTERS AND A MADMAN

EVE TARRINGTON

TENACIOUS TEACUP PRESS

*For my family*

**1**

———————

"Miss St Clair," said Mr Percival Haddington ever so gently. "You have every reason in the world to think ill of me. But I pray you would let my wife decide for herself."

Judith tried not to look at her friend's brother. "As one who is charged with protecting her, I cannot allow that. And you, yourself, should be very well aware that we do not have visitors. Certain friends—a group of three women who volunteer and are chosen by a special committee. That is all."

She looked up at the tall brick building. It did not look like a madhouse, but it was no ordinary home. And though Judith should have been kind to the husband, who stood there with his hat in his hands, begging for admittance, Mrs. Peggy Haddington would be much better off without the sight of him. In fact, Judith did not even mean to tell her that the man had visited.

The warm summer day had just enough of a breeze to blow the occasional cloud across the sun and make working in the garden tolerable. Judith was only sweating because it rarely fell upon her to keep the more determined visitors away, and she was not at all sure she would be able to do it.

"Come," said Mr Haddington, giving her a sad smile.

Judith could not help but note that he looked remarkably well. The last time she had seen him, he had been newly released from prison, very thin, and prone to fits.

"Surely, given the circumstances, your superintendent would be inclined to make an exception."

Judith frowned, looking back over at her charge. Mercy was deep in the grips of melancholia, but still, the promise of the sunshine had been enough to get her out of her bed and down the stairs. Judith wondered whether Mercy would not soon start to pull the carrots out of the garden again if she did not find her something to eat. Their superintendent was always going on about the importance of food. Judith, who had been raised in a family that put a great emphasis on thrift, thought it madness to have meat daily—at times, more than once a day—and cheese after every meal. But she knew that without food, Mercy would be worse.

"Mr Haddington." Judith faced him. "Of course our superintendent, I am sure, is most inclined to be thankful for everything he has received from your family. But please do not forget he is just as solicitous of your wife's comfort as I am. He will not take kindly to your coming here."

"What? Would you call me no more than a disturbance?" Mr Haddington drew himself up. "I do not need to ask you whether my wife still loves me. We were made for each other, she and I, and if it took me many years to realise it, you can call me no worse than a fool."

"One could say many things." Even in her anger, Judith was not about to think up epithets to hurl at her friend's husband. "But I have plenty to report when it comes to your wife. Because of your cruel neglect and your unwillingness to speak the truths that might have saved you, she arrived here in such a state that she could hardly walk. For days, she was either trembling or weeping, and for months, she did not smile. If your cousin Mr Ephraim Ramsbury had not gone on so often about the cruelty of madhouses, I have no doubt she would have ended up at Bethlem or some worse place."

"But she did not." Mr Haddington turned pale. "I would never have allowed—"

"You were not part of the party that accompanied her here. Though I am proud to call myself Peggy's friend at this time, I was nearly a stranger then, and still, I saw fit to accompany her."

"I did not wish to distress her further!" he said. "There were plenty of reasons for that. I was not at all recovered myself."

Judith saw that Mercy was trying to pull a cabbage out of the ground, and she ran over. "We do not need that for the soup again," she said softly but firmly. "Perhaps if you would be so good as to gather some of the dill? I am sure it will be needed later this evening."

Mercy nodded and put down the cabbage. She made no move toward the dill, only sat in the dirt like an exhausted child. Judith thought she should have brought bonnets for both of them. It was sunny enough that they would surely be tan if she were not cautious.

"Peggy would have had feet rotting from cold, wrapped in flannel against the horrid temperatures." The crackling sound in Judith's voice reminded her that it had been too long since she had taken refreshment. Perhaps Mercy would consent to go sit under the willow tree awhile if Judith could procure some tea for both of them.

"But instead, she is here and well. That is why—"

"You say 'well' as if it were the final word. She can manage all the ladies under her care and with a deft hand. That is true enough. But she still has nightmares. Still dislikes to speak with anyone who is not a very intimate friend. Even when we have the visitors I spoke of, she is very nearly silent. And you have yourself to thank for all that. She is not as strong as she was, and the doctor tells us that we should never expect her to make a full recovery."

She looked over at Mercy, who was staring at the door above the steps leading to the garden.

"The doctor has not told me such a thing," said the lady standing in front of the door. She was plumper than Judith, and her face was beautiful, but it wore a sad expression that did not match the arch tone she had taken.

"Peggy," said Judith, rushing over. "I am so sorry. Only I was hoping to make him leave, and—"

"You need not make him do anything, Judith," said her friend, looking only at her husband. "If I ask him to leave, he certainly shall."

Mr Percival Haddington looked pale. "You would ask that of me?"

"Yes," she said. "I certainly hope our friend Judith was not correct in every particular, but I can say with absolute certainty that I do not wish you here."

2

———

Mercy did not need her own attendant, Judith had decided. That is, she did need attention from only one person, but it was impossible to tell when the mania would strike her. At those times, it was a trial to keep her safe, and coaxing her conversation into something besides loud and laugh-filled ramblings was nearly impossible. When she was taken by the melancholia, however, she could be with nearly anyone with little threat of harm.

So she was happy to sit on the porch of the superintendent's home while Judith asked his wife about the work.

"I ought to have got Mercy beyond this stage by now," Judith lamented. "I have been with her for months."

"Is she within hearing?" asked Margaret Lamb gently.

Judith went to the window. Nobody in the establishment was ever more careful not to speak of guests within their hearing than Margaret, the wife of their superintendent. Though her husband, Thomas, and their doctor, Jeremiah Murray, claimed it was important, Judith had noticed both of them breaking the rules, particularly in those rare but terrifying moments when the violence of a person's mind was turned against any unfortunate soul who happened to be about. While Judith still shied away in those moments, her friend Peggy's face became set and strong. Judith thought with shame of what she had said. Yes, Peggy Haddington was weak in certain ways, but she was much better at dealing with the fire of others' spirits than Judith had ever been, even after over a year spent learning.

When she saw that Mercy might be able to hear them, she spoke more quietly. It was too hot to close the window.

"I think Mercy would do quite well under Peggy's care," Judith said to Margaret. "Only, I can tell when she is slipping, and I know that Bach will continue to calm her. Even if it is not the first choice of anyone else here."

"Because nobody else loves Bach as you do, dear," said Margaret, "you must stay with her. It is the closest thing we have to a cure, and it is sacred music. It is not frivolous."

"No," said Judith, and she saw that the older woman was uncommonly restless. She kept rising to go look out into her own passageway then coming back to her chair. As the female superintendent, she was responsible for the overall welfare of the women, but she was not solely responsible for any of them. Judith could not think of a time when she had ever seen Margaret Lamb so uneasy.

"I am sorry." Margaret furrowed her brow. "But I must attend to a few things, Judith. You must come visit us more often. Since you and Peggy left, you have hardly been to dinner once, even when there are other ladies who can be spared."

Judith looked down at her feet, counting the worst of the scuff marks in her shoes. Though she had not intentionally come with plain dress in mind, she was adhering to the principle of both wearing simple clothes and of wearing her clothes until they were too worn out to be used as garments. She did not wish to reject the hospitality, yet she had her reasons for avoiding the dinners. To her, they were something to be dreaded every bit as much as she had hated the society affairs her friend Louisa-Margaretta Haddington used to make her attend.

At least with Louisa-Margaretta, she'd always had the fun of her friend's company. Even if rich and titled neighbors made Judith hold her tongue, Louisa-Margaretta had no such compunctions and, at least once every dinner, greatly offended at least one of their guests by pointing out some absurdity. Once, she had told the second Chandler son quite plainly that the Haddingtons had been warned upon their arrival in the neighborhood to leave him out of dinners. Everyone said that he was so ill-mannered with the women that he would ruin their parties. Judith was amused to see that the young man, in spite of the wine he had drunk, immediately recognised the truth of her remarks and took care to alter his manner for the rest of the evening.

The dinners with the Lamb family were worse—all the difficulties of socializing with none of the fun.

"I am sure I should come soon," Judith said, and she lowered her voice again. "Only, I do like to see that Mercy is eating. You know what the doctor says about food."

Margaret at last gave her full attention to Judith once more, frowning. "You think she will not be well provisioned in your absence?"

"No, only that I have observed that Mercy must be with a familiar companion, or she may not eat well. She may accept only the daintiest bites of food, then she will not sleep."

At that, Margaret sighed. "Perhaps I can ask Bathsheba to do something about that. She could use a distraction."

They both rose.

"Has Bathsheba not been well since her journey?" Judith asked. "I know the passage can be a trying one. I have never made it myself, but that is what I have heard."

"Yes," said Margaret before she nearly collided with a figure in the doorway.

Judith gave the superintendent a strained smile and a nod. "Good morning," she said before she could stop herself.

Thomas Lamb smiled, but his eyes were steady. "Judith Clair, I see we have not convinced thee to leave off such greetings."

Judith stopped smiling and immediately apologised. "I have forgotten again," she said. "I am a slow study, and I am terribly sorry. Soon, I shall learn this better. I promise."

In fact, she had learned after a month not to say "Good morning" or "Good evening" to the Quakers she met, and after many more months had passed, she rarely made a mistake. But with the superintendent, she made all sorts of mistakes, and she was not prepared to say in her own defense that he was the cause of them. If only he had not distracted her with the way he said her name. Most of the residents were happy to call her Judith, using the Quaker custom of addressing everyone by their first name. But Thomas Lamb seemed determined to call her by her full name. Only, her surname, St Clair, was blasphemous to those who did not believe in sainthood. So he called her Judith Clair, and she found herself galled by the omission in spite of her efforts to smile and forget.

"Margaret, where is Bathsheba? We have a full complement, and she is not to think she can give in to idleness simply because she is still tired from her journey."

"I will find her," she said gently, but that seemed only to aggravate the man.

"Yes, well, I will be off seeing to William," he said as if he were the only person in the place putting his mind to useful tasks.

**3**

———

"I will go speak to my daughter," said Margaret. "Judith, I wish you and Mercy a very pleasant morning."

Behind her, a young woman slipped out the door and walked over to the opposite side of the porch. "Judith, Mercy," she said in greeting, sighing as if the very act of speaking exhausted her.

"Don't lurk there," said Margaret, her voice stern but warm. "It's not polite."

"If I lurk in my bed, it will be called sloth, and I will have to get up." Bathsheba folded herself into a chair on the opposite side of the porch.

Neither of them mentioned the superintendent.

"I was just leaving," said Judith.

"No, thou was just telling Mama what happened with Peggy." Bathsheba's face looked as if it had faded since she went away, and while Judith was thankful that she had come back, she wondered why the Lambs had sent her off at all. Perhaps the superintendents' daughter could not be allowed to have a touch of melancholia. It was rather too close to weakness.

"Well, it wasn't with Peggy, quite," said Judith. She did not know why she objected to telling both of them. Margaret represented safety to her, a perfect confidante.

Bathsheba, on the other hand, was perfect with the most difficult patients. Sometimes, she laughed, and other times, she cried, but it all seemed to have a better effect than if she had simply been calm. Perhaps people responded to her youth and unstudied emotion. But it made her more difficult for Judith to speak with somehow.

"It was her husband, Percival Haddington," Judith said, and the older woman's lips tightened.

"He should not have spoken to any of our ladies," she said. "Thou may scream for us if he tries again, of course. He ought to have known better. A young lady—"

Judith straightened, horrified. "Oh, it was nothing of that sort!"

Margaret still looked skeptical.

Judith tripped over her words as she tried to explain. "He says that he still loves Peggy and wants her to come away with him," she said, struck by the unpleasant sensation that the jilted husband's feelings had seemed sincere enough. Then again, it Peggy was the one who had been jilted. Of course, that word was not strong enough. She had been betrayed.

"She was at her weakest—well, you both saw her when she came a year ago. It was just before thou left." Judith glanced at Bathsheba. She looked uncharacteristically rattled, as if she already expected everyone to have forgotten she had been gone.

"Peggy went through many dark months when she first

arrived," said Margaret. "We were blessed that thou accompanied her, Judith."

"I am quite sure we could have managed." Bathsheba frowned. "We have good men and women. We have a doctor."

Margaret, with uncustomary annoyance, gave her daughter a sharp look.

Judith apologised. "I am sorry. I do not mean to imply that there was anything wanting. Only that Peggy had a terrible time of it and she will never go back to her former self. I tried to make Mr... I mean, Percival Haddington... understand that she is still not well completely. Oh, well enough to care for everyone but not to have to argue with the man who lied to her before abandoning her most cruelly."

"She is hardly a child," said Bathsheba, who looked like a child herself, though she was no longer as thin as she had been before her journey. Perhaps her relatives had a more permissive view of rich food. "Should not Peggy be the judge?"

"If she wanted to return to him, she easily could have before now," said Judith. "She has found peace here. As have I."

"Speaking of which, have you thought about where you will be headed afterwards, Judith?" Margaret asked. "You came, as I understand, to help Peggy and make sure she was well cared for. Anyone can see that you managed the task with great devotion."

"And now I ought to be done. Is that what you are saying?"

Judith chastised herself for forgetting "thou" again, but Bathsheba did not appear to notice. The younger Lamb walked over to the porch railing and stared into the woods.

"One ought not to keep families from coming together is all," she said. "It is not natural to keep them apart, not when the love is there."

**4**

─────

"It is not natural for families to be so long parted, surely," said Federica Gillingham, giving Louisa-Margaretta a puzzled smile. "Surely you do not intend to stay in town beyond this season."

"As long as there are husbands aplenty, I will stay here until I have found one," said Louisa-Margaretta cooly. "And since I have not, I am sure that I may be here well beyond this season."

"But, Louie," said Federica, calling her the pet name she had used since their nursery days, "you have had plenty of offers already. If it were only the wish for a husband that kept you here, why did you reject them all?"

Louisa-Margaretta looked about the ballroom then forced her eyes to drift back to her friend. Having to talk about the suitors she had rejected was humiliating.

"First, there was that lovely count," said Federica.

"He was poor. I don't want to be a prize for a fortune hunter."

"But his pedigree, Louie! He was hardly garden variety, and I think you may have broken his heart."

Louisa-Margaretta, feeling rather than seeing eyes that were focused on her, turned toward her friend. "You can't say I learned nothing from him. I tried to keep the next ones from getting any ideas of marriage."

"But Mr Hann—"

"Thick. You know that. I could never marry a stupid man."

"And Mr Stephen Pratt?"

"Younger son. Again, poor. Though he was smarter than Mr Hann. I will give you that."

"So you are here to find some sort of romantic ideal?"

It would not be for Federica Gillingham to understand that particular ambition. She had married young, one of the first of Louisa-Margaretta's circle of friends to leave the fold. Her husband was a man Louisa-Margaretta used to call "Donald the Dull," and as far as she could see, that name only grew more accurate as they all grew older. By the time Louisa-Margaretta had been banished to the countryside, Federica already had three children and a decided weariness for London society. She would have liked the country better, she had confessed. She liked her children and her needlework well enough and did not need the fashions of town to entertain her. Strangely enough, she even seemed to enjoy the company of her husband. But Louisa-Margaretta did not want a sister-in-law for a chaperone, so Federica had accompanied her to ball after ball. And if she did not marry soon, she would be forced to search the town for someone half as obliging, as another confinement was nearing for her friend, and even the earliest parties were proving rather tiring.

"I am not looking for a romantic ideal," said Louisa-Margaretta, thinking of the season when she had been in love. It felt as if it had been at least a decade ago, though it had only been two years.

She would never again meet a man as agreeable as Isaac, who conformed to her romantic notions in every way. He had gone off to Amsterdam, she heard, where he hoped to make his fortune. She'd heard little else, because she did not want to hear that he had married, so she never asked. To think that he could be living a quiet life similar to Federica's, with a spouse the family approved of and children who had his eyes, was an insult she tried not to dwell on.

Though in moments when her mind was idle, she returned to it, and she had to rely on her company to distract her.

"Look at how that older gentleman is dressed," she said wearily. "I have never understood why anyone would wear a powdered wig. One almost expects him to draw out a sword."

"Oh, Louie," said Federica, laughing in spite of herself. "Will we not insist on the fashions of our youth when we ourselves are old ladies?"

"These are classical silhouettes," said Louisa-Margaretta, looking down at her fine gown, its green color chosen specially to set off the red in her hair. "Who is to say that they will ever be out of fashion?"

"It is unlike you to sound naive," said Federica. "Our gowns are more comfortable than our mothers' or grandmothers' were, and you can be certain that the future will bring a return to some sort of discomfort. We cannot be allowed to move freely."

"Why not?"

"Because we are ladies," said Federica placidly. "Our clothing will always be uncomfortable, particularly when it is fine. It is only a matter of degree."

When Louisa-Margaretta made no answer, Federica added gently, "Perhaps that is your own view on marriage, and this is why you have not said yes to any of the suitors?"

Louisa-Margaretta gazed around the room, which held many young men, handsome ones, and smiles were not in short supply. But she could not think of how to state what she wished in a husband without insulting her friend's choice.

"He needs to have a strong character," she said. "He need not be in love with me, but he must be secure in his choice."

Federica frowned. "Surely you do not think any of the young men I have mentioned were not sure about their wishes. They were all most sincere."

"Yes, and they all moved on to other young ladies shortly after I did not show interest in them."

"Well, what would you have them do? A man who does not accept a young lady's wishes is a boor."

"One may accept them, to be sure. But if my husband is to be steady over the years, no matter what befalls us, the attachment must be based upon more than a passing fancy, whether it is love or love of money. That is all."

"And you are sure that this is not an excuse?"

"To stay unmarried?"

"To stay true to your first love."

Silence followed, and Federica touched her friend's arm. "Do not think that I blame you. I was not touched in the same way, but I do not think it is unreasonable, Louie."

"Look what happened to Percival." Louisa's tone was hard. "Though Peggy was my favourite, and though there was love there, as soon as obstacles came between them, each of them completely lost their heads. And he betrayed her because his love was too weak to see the woman he loved sink into madness."

"Louie," said Federica quietly.

"I was there," she said, her voice growing louder. "And I can assure you she would not have been half so mad had Percival not abandoned her."

"Louie," said Federica again. "I really think—"

"You will make the excuse that Percival was weak in all respects, not just this one. And I would say that this hardly matters. If your affection or duty to your spouse is not enough to make you overcome some innate weakness of character, well, the marriage is doomed. And that is why I will not accept any of these suitors, not until I can be sure that they would do something differently. My brother, in his foolishness—"

"Louisa-Margaretta," said Federica sharply.

Turning, Louisa-Margaretta found her brother standing next to them, his face cold and set.

"Good evening, dear," he said. "Pray, don't let me interrupt."

**5**

---

"What are you doing here?" asked Louisa-Margaretta.

"Picking up where your chaperone has been neglecting her duty," he growled. "I shall have to speak to Mama about you using poor Mrs. Gillingham for your own ends."

Louisa-Margaretta bristled. "Nobody is being used, I assure you."

"She has failed to keep you away from unsavory gentlemen, and that means you have lost even the appearance of respectability."

At that, Louisa-Margaretta laughed, perhaps too loudly. "Percival, dearest, you must have just arrived. I have not so much as spoken to a gentleman since my arrival here, and I certainly have not been dancing. If standing in a ballroom in close conference with a married lady is scandalous, I am afraid you will have to punish most of the ladies here for such an indiscretion."

He glowered at her. "Mr Fortescue has been looking at you a great deal."

Louisa-Margaretta listened with amusement. She did not share the popular view of Mr Fortescue. To most members of high society, he was to be courted carefully or else avoided. He had a reputation as a rake, to the point that he likely would have been banished from polite company were it not for his very old family name and his extensive property. Most chaperones allowed their young ladies to dance with him once but no more, and they would be very careful to make sure of his intentions before allowing him to proceed in turning the head of any lady.

In spite of those intentions, of course, he turned a great deal of heads. Mr Fortescue had looks that were at once devastatingly handsome and quite unusual—even exotic. And that he treated all the young women he met with indifference at best did nothing to hurt his case with them. Rather, they fawned over the handsome man who barely deigned to speak to them. Even the clever ones were not immune.

Mr Fortescue's features were sharp but regular, dark, aristocratic, and gorgeous. Some said his father had been a successful trader, coming all the way from China to eventually settle in London, where he made a vast fortune and married a young lady from one of the best families. The father was still alive, but the mother had died in childbirth with her third child, a daughter. Rumours floated around that Mr Fortescue's motherless upbringing was the reason he did not wish to marry, though apparently, both his younger brother and his sister had married well.

Louisa-Margaretta glanced over at him, and though she was surprised to meet his eyes, she did not choose to look away. He was handsome, to be sure, but that was not the only thing that made her shiver. His gaze was direct, filled with a hunger that reeked of both imprudence and intrigue.

No other man had ever looked at her in that way, and even though she was determined not to drop her gaze, she ended up turning back to her brother as her neck flushed.

"This is exactly what I mean," growled Percival, who had missed none of it. "I need to get you away from such men. Surely you do not think yourself an exception, Louisa-Margaretta. That gentleman, if I am forced to refer to him as such, can hardly have honourable intentions."

"I can take care of myself, thank you very much."

"But if you insist on staying—"

"You cannot very well force me to leave. And if I may say it, Percival, you do not exactly help your case by coming into this ballroom and telling me that I am a naive little idiot. In fact, I would be quite happy to leave London and travel with some degree of freedom but not in the company of one who sees me as a child."

Louisa-Margaretta tried not to allow her voice to betray her. When she thought of leaving the city, her body felt heavy with relief. Many of her friends had already left, seeking the amusements of the seaside or the comfort of country estates, and she had stayed on because she could not bear the thought of going back to Wycliff Castle, her parents' house in Derbyshire. The more she had grown to love the independence of being a woman who was unmarried, the more she resented the strictures that were placed on her as a spinster. Federica had suggested gently that as a married woman with the right husband, Louisa-Margaretta would be allowed a great deal more independence, and she was beginning to agree. The trouble was that in order to marry, she had to keep doing the rounds of eligible gentlemen, and she was not sure how much longer she could bear it.

She hardly noticed that Percival was apologizing.

"I thought this was the best way," he said. "But really, I came because I need your help. Again."

"I am sure. But given that I am hardly able to look after myself, how can I be expected to help you?"

"It is a matter of the heart," he said with sudden sincerity that she could not ignore. "You see, it is about Peggy."

"A matter of the heart?" came a quiet but powerful voice over his shoulder. "My dear Mr Haddington, how fascinating. I would love to hear of it after you introduce me to your sister."

And together, the Haddingtons turned to face Mr Fortescue, who had come over to them and was looking with an expectant smirk at the man who had once been his companion in sampling the many delights of London.

**6**

———

Judith blamed her poor night on her argument with Mr Percival Haddington. It had caused Peggy to get angry with her and later made the Lambs quite withdrawn. Bathsheba Lamb had been uncharacteristically brusque toward Judith when she talked about Judith's plans to continue the separation of the Haddingtons, who had once been bound by affection.

*That is not what I wanted anyway,* thought Judith as she blew out her candle.

The home did not like to spend the fees of their subscribers on more light than was necessary, though they also did not believe in locking anyone up in dark rooms during the day. Sometimes, when she had her half day, Judith went down to the village and bought her own candles. Her sleep was still often troubled, and she liked being permitted to stay awake longer than the frugal nature of her employers might have allowed.

Mercy seemed tired enough after her long meal in the evening, but before daybreak, she grew restless. That was the trouble with summer, Judith had decided. Others might love the long days and sunlight, but Mercy always stirred before sunrise. That meant very short nights of rest for her minder.

Because Judith was Mercy's primary companion—at the home, they did not encourage use of the term "nurse"—she slept in an adjoining room. The doors between the rooms locked. Judith had a key for Mercy's safety if she was having a fit, but she had never used it. Generally, they slept with the door open and a great deal of blankets on each bed.

Mercy was up and pacing in the wee hours, making low moans. If Peggy had been there, she might have helped Mercy back to bed, where she would have tried to soothe her with stories as one might soothe a fractious child. Of course, at the home, they were encouraged to choose stories from the Bible, but Judith noticed that Peggy often told stories from her childhood. One was about finding a lost horse and seemed a particular source of comfort, though Judith could not have said whether it was true. She knew that Peggy had not been happy with her family, and her marriage to Mr Percival Haddington was an escape. Although she had known even then that she would not have children in such a marriage because of a physical defect of Percival's, she had agreed because she was poor and unhappy. Or so Percival claimed. Judith was not sure what parts of his account were true, just as she could not be sure whether Peggy had been rewarded with candy for finding a runaway mare as a child.

After months with Mercy, Judith knew that the stories would not work. They had never worked for Peggy. When Mercy was awake and it was near dawn, she was not likely to sleep again. The two of them might as well go out.

"Mercy, choose a dress," Judith said gently.

It had taken her some time to bring Mercy away from

the well-respected custom of plain dress. That custom was strange to Judith at times, as she saw plenty of the ladies who came to visit wearing clothes with simple designs made of exceedingly fine material. Even Bathsheba liked to use silk and ribbon whenever she thought she could get away with it. Both of the elder Lambs were adamant about plain dress on themselves and the people they cared for, but Judith had been persuasive. Mercy had always loved fine clothes, and like Peggy, she had not been a Quaker before she came to the home. Her husband said that he had only joined after she went mad, as he could no longer abide the answers he was getting from rectors and vicars who saw madness as punishment for sin.

When Mercy was allowed to choose her own clothes, she invariably chose either a rich-green gown or a yellow dress with lots of ribbons. The other three dresses available to her were exceedingly plain. She had a larger wardrobe than most anyone at the home saw fit to maintain, but Judith had argued that the choice of clothing was an essential one for Mercy. And indeed, at times, having her choose a costume and stand still as Judith played lady's maid and dressed her was the only way to keep her calm.

Mercy had chosen the yellow dress, and Judith was glad. Perhaps the color would raise her spirits, although it was so early that they both had to wear coats.

They went out into the open portion of the garden. Judith hoped that Mercy would be content to wander and that she would not run. In Judith's earliest days at the home, she had not been able to keep pace with Mercy, and even Peggy had struggled. But as their time there wore on, Peggy and Judith both grew stronger and faster. Mercy, on the other hand, seemed to grow weaker. Judith was always trying to get her to eat more, mostly without success. And

Judith herself had never eaten better than she did at the home. When she knew that she had to set an example for the other ladies, showing a healthy appetite and excellent manners, she was rarely tempted to eat less simply because of her ill temper, as she'd once had. She was stouter and healthier than she had been since her mother's death.

And she was faster, which was just as well. Mercy had started running.

## 7

Judith knew better than to chase Mercy by running behind her. That would only spur her on. At times, they had seriously considered looking for a shepherd who could lend them a dog. At least such a creature would be able to keep up with Mercy, and herding powers might even be necessary.

Judith had become able to keep up, only there was always danger in the field. With the way Mercy tried to run across it, as straight and sure as any horse, the slightest hill or dip could be enough to break her leg.

Judith made a wide loop, coming around Mercy, then stood with her hands in front of her.

Mercy always respected obstacles, and she stopped. Judith offered her arm, and they walked back together.

Mercy's face was expressionless, though her cheeks were pink. Judith, breathing hard from the exertion, wished she could ask Mercy why she had run. She had often asked Margaret.

"There was a case of a man—or a boy, really, who came

to us. He was able to explain most things. But he said he could not tell us why he ran," Margaret had explained.

"Could not or would not tell you?" said Judith.

"Could not. He wished to run, and he found that wish impossible to resist. Although eventually, he did manage to resist it."

"How? Was there some sort of promise involved? Food?"

"No, nothing of that sort. One day, a farmer's bull got loose and gave him a nasty scare. After that, he never ran again," Margaret said.

Judith blinked. "I don't suppose—"

"Dear Judith, of course not. We couldn't put Mercy's life at risk."

From Margaret's tone, Judith knew this was meant to be final.

"Not even to save her life?"

"When there is someone to run after her, her life will be well protected."

*This is true enough,* Judith reflected with a sad smile at her charge. Ever since Judith had insisted that Mercy have one sole companion, the poor thing had never managed to get more than a hundred yards away when she was running.

Judith chastised herself for using *poor thing* even in her thoughts, but she could not help but pity Mercy. She must be subject to the same whims and passions that governed every other man and woman at the home. But unlike all the rest, Mercy was never able to speak of anything. Judith wondered who Mercy had been in the days when she could speak, before she had lost so many of her faculties. She had always asked about how it had happened, but not even Bathsheba Lamb would speak of it.

"Oh, how can thou ask something so painful? It is the worst sort of gossip!" Bathsheba had cried. She was a young woman who always loved to discuss the particulars of those who came to stay with them, who thrived on Judith's visits precisely because she longed for speculative conversations. And not only did Bathsheba seem to know something of the subject, but she objected to Judith's asking about it.

"I know that you were once a rather fine lady," said Judith to Mercy. "And you still are. But a lady must think of her skirts before running through the grass when it is still cold with dew."

Mercy's face was unreadable.

Judith could not help correcting herself. "I could have said 'thou.' But I know that you were not a Quaker before, and I am not sure 'thou' would be preferable. And to be quite honest, I do not prefer it, Mercy."

The woman made a queer sort of gurgling sound.

Judith lowered her voice now that they were closer to the garden, as she did not want to wake anyone who might have had a difficult time sleeping during the night. "I do not object to the principle, you understand. I am sure we are all quite equal in God's eyes. Only, having been used to saying things one way all my life, I have found it rather trying to adopt this new language."

Another strange sound followed. Judith looked at Mercy with some alarm. She lowered her voice again without thinking. After many months of speaking in a near whisper when another was yelling at her, Judith was very used to speaking quietly.

"I will hush now, Mercy," she said in tones that she hoped were soothing. "I am very sorry to have upset you."

But then she heard the sound again, and it was a piercing cry, one that was coming from a basket Judith had nearly tripped over, not from Mercy.

**8**

———————

Judith reached for the baby, and she was holding the bundle of the child and its blanket before she remembered Mercy was with her. For the first time that morning, she could read Mercy's face easily. She was giving a smile of wonder. Mercy drew close, touching the child's cheek, and suddenly, she had the calm expression of a Madonna captured by an ancient painter.

Judith was scarcely breathing. She had seen babies that were abandoned, of course, because some of them were left at churches. But she never imagined she would see one in an institution for people who had been deemed mad. She wondered what sort of mother would trust strangers afflicted by madness with such a small, defenseless child.

But there was no time for speculation. The gurgling resumed, and the baby began to squirm in Judith's arms. With a start, she realised the babe must be hungry, and she was going to need help with feeding if she was also to make sure that Mercy did not run off. She looked longingly across the grass. The little brick building beckoned to her, but even though the morning would be warm, she did not like to keep the baby out in the air any longer than she must.

The trouble was solved for her when she saw Margaret walking across the meadow. Seeing the female superintendent coming and going was not out of the ordinary. She, even more than her husband or the doctor, never shied away from the men and women who were angry or sad. And she did not wait for problems to arise but came and went at all hours, bringing her air of competence and composure.

But it was a bit unusual to see her walking so quickly. Margaret never hurried. Even when she needed to move quickly, she did not tend to rush. Judith had been in more than one crisis in which she remembered Margaret telling her to breathe. "Keep things slow and keep others from gathering. Make sure it is not too bright or too loud. Then and only then can thou bring in something sweet."

That had been her advice on Judith's first full day at the home, when Judith was struggling to help a distraught young woman.

"Something sweet?" Judith had asked, flinching away from Deborah, the young woman who was screaming herself hoarse. She thought that "sweetness" must be another one of the religious concepts she had not yet mastered.

"Like a slice of cake," said Margaret gently. "Or tea in china cups. I will stay, if thou wilt go to the kitchen now."

Judith did so and was given all the things an elegant tea party would require. As soon as she saw the cups, she envisioned them smashed on the floor. She told Margaret as much in a whisper, though when she came back in, Deborah was at least pacing and moaning, not screaming.

"I would not wish to be offered tea by an indifferent hostess," Margaret said placidly. "When we are expecting a lady to bring her best self to the table, the table must look its best."

Judith had commented on the services they had many times since. Plainness was such a virtue, at least for the people who had created the home, that she was surprised to see the cups with elegant patterns and handles that were just as decorative as they were functional.

"My husband does not approve of them," Margaret confessed. "And we do have two plain sets, if one of our guests or our visitors insists. We do want to respect their wishes, after all."

Judith remembered how so many people of her acquaintance had only wished for the plainest dishes. It was easier to replace a plain dish than a patterned one, after all, and even in the household where she had been raised, certain patterns were considered rather ostentatious.

"None of them have ever been smashed, Judith," Margaret explained. "I cannot speak for the men, of course, but to the women, this is exactly the sort of cup that demands respect. And respect is the greatest gift we have."

This morning, Margaret was walking with her plain skirt clutched in her worn hands, rushing forward without any of her customary aplomb.

"Mercy," she said. "That is not thy child."

Judith looked up in surprise. "Of course not," she said. "But Mercy is ever so good with the little one."

She meant it too. Where she felt awkward and uncertain, Mercy's touches were gentle and sure. She was stroking the infant's head with a self-possession that surprised Judith. Though Judith had held Miriam and certainly all of her younger brothers, she had never much liked the months that came before they were able to raise their heads and make noises at her. Infants, she had concluded, were simply too small and helpless. They were a trial that had to be endured, and why every mother and father she met seemed to lose their hearts to them remained a mystery. Judith much preferred older children.

"Mercy," said Margaret again. "Please, it is not safe. Let Judith give her to me."

Mercy gave the slightest shake of her head. She was smiling down at the infant, rocking from side to side ever so slowly.

Judith found herself in the unfamiliar position of having to reassure the female superintendent. "It is safe," she insisted. "This child is more beautiful than the finest piece of china. Dost not thou agree? The child demands our respect."

In fact, Judith could not quite think of the infant as beautiful, but her words seemed to resonate with Margaret, who stepped back. She looked in the direction of the house she shared with some of the guests, which surprised Judith. Now that they had the attention of one of their leaders, surely they would not need any more help.

"I will go for milk," said Judith. "We must feed the little one."

"I will go," said Margaret. "We must have boiled milk for her."

Mercy still did not move, and Judith looked nervously back at the home. She had never taken a great interest in infants, but she knew some of them did not like spoons and rags when they were in their tenderest days.

"Might we not find a wife from the village, someone with milk to spare?" she asked. "This baby seems a delicate thing."

"No," said Margaret. "Give her to me. I can take her

straight to the kitchens. Then she will return with me, and I will look after her."

Mercy looked downcast as Judith placed the baby in Margaret's arms. "I am not certain," said Judith, hesitating. "Perhaps I could go to the village. Maybe Peggy or Bathsheba could help me."

"No," said Margaret. "It is not necessary. Judith, Mercy, you go on in. If you want to see the child, I will bring her to you soon."

Judith said nothing more, though she felt there was something odd in both Mercy's and Margaret's manners. Mercy was moving more slowly and deliberately than Judith had ever seen. Margaret stared at the child, rooted to the spot.

"Come, Mercy," said Judith, but the cry of the little one continued to disturb her.

She would have to see to it that the mite did not go hungry, Margaret's insistence on isolation notwithstanding. If she had learned anything at the home, it was that one must always take care to eat well.

9

---

At first, Judith could not insist on a wet nurse, but after some days had passed, she tried to reason with Margaret again. She could sense Mercy's moods easily enough and knew that an afternoon in which Mercy was pleased with the luncheon at the Lambs' would be as safe a time as any. The doctor would not be joining them, so that also made her task easier. When Mercy snapped from gladness straight to anger, it was most often because of his interference.

But she still had Lucy from the kitchen keep an eye on her just in case. As soon as Judith and Mercy arrived at the home the superintendents shared with the most sociable guests, Judith sought Lucy out.

"What am I to do with her?" asked Lucy, her eyes watering from the smoke that had begun to overtake the room.

Margaret, far from being an elegant lady who wished her daughters to keep away from her cooking, had insisted that Bathsheba learn. That had always been something of the joke in the family, as Bathsheba had been an indifferent cook at best. But since her travels, her cookery had gone from merely plain to rather terrible. Food was either raw, burned, or completely forgotten, and Mary, their cook, had already threatened to leave if Bathsheba could not be kept out of the kitchen. Bathsheba, of course, had little wish to cook, but even when her mother did not enforce the rule, her father had adopted the philosophy behind it. He thought it best that his daughter not become one of those "useless, mincing women" who could not lift a finger and wished she would be like the honorable wife of the Old Testament, putting her skills to use for her husband and family.

Of course, Bathsheba did not have a husband and had often complained of that before her journey. Peggy, running away from hers, and Judith, determined to keep the home as a sort of personal nunnery, had both disliked Bathsheba's speeches on the subject. Since Bathsheba's return, she had not complained about her unmarried state. Judith wondered if the time with her mother's family was supposed to be a window in which Bathsheba might find her way into a marriage. If that had failed, perhaps she had come home disheartened.

With a pang, Judith thought of Louisa-Margaretta. Her friend wished to marry. Even before Peggy had begun writing back, she received long, affectionate letters from her mother-in-law, ones that Judith read eagerly for news of her family. The elder Mrs. Haddington was deeply worried— that much was plain—and it was unlike her to stay buried in the countryside while her daughter was chaperoned about London by women whose experience and wits might not be up to the task. Louisa-Margaretta must have had quite a plan for forcing her mother to stay away. Judith imagined she had threatened the family with a second scandal. When last they met, Louisa-Margaretta had been so determined to get free of her family that Judith was sure she would not return to Wycliff Castle even if it meant her unhappiness.

Judith made her excuses as the Lambs were sitting down to their light luncheon with select visitors amongst them. She was always uncomfortable with the meals she took with the superintendents and their daughter. Those visitors who were of the best sort, of course, and paid full fees, would be sitting down to table as well, unless they were indisposed. Even if they had to come over from the other building, dining with the superintendents' family on every delicacy that could be reasonably got in for them was something they were permitted to take for granted. The male superintendent, of course, thought the meals were "greatly beneficial" for those from the lower classes who were showing some improvements. "For them to have a meal in better circumstances than they might otherwise expect, sharing a table and conversation with those whose society they might experience but rarely, can only be of great benefit."

Though Margaret never directly contradicted her husband in that respect, Judith noticed that she did not speak of the benefit as being solely something that went to the poorer guests at the table. She had noted more than once that ladies and gentlemen who were used to seeing their every eccentricity tolerated, even honored, by overindulgent families often behaved better if they saw elegant guests whose good breeding meant a great deal more than their lack of fortune.

Lucy grudgingly gave Judith some bread and cheese to eat as she sought out a large tree where Peggy had taken the little one for a bit of milk and fresh air.

"She's still not drinking as she ought, poor love," Peggy said without looking at Judith, wiggling a rag that had been dipped in milk into the baby's mouth. "I can't think how she is happy in spite of it all. Margaret says she is getting plenty, and I suppose she must be, though if every feeding is like this one, I cannot see how."

The baby still looked thin, but her cheeks seemed the tiniest bit fuller.

At first, Judith was too nervous to speak, but seeing the little thing made her calm enough to offer up one thought. "It would be best to find a woman who can nurse her. My mother did it for babies who were poorly, especially after she lost a child. She said it made all the difference."

Peggy wrapped her arms around the little bundle, casting a protective look up at Judith. "I am not sure it is for you to decide, Judith."

Judith could see that Peggy was regretting her comments. No doubt she preferred to deal with Margaret, not the young woman who had once been her minder.

Judith sighed. "Of course not. But why should any of us decide? We all found the child, even if the nursery is here with the Lambs. I am not sure they should tell us how she should be fed, especially since it must be ages since any of them has cared for an infant."

"Well, I never have, and it has been some years for you too. Though your youngest brother is very young."

Her smile was sly, and Judith accepted it. Though she found Joseph to be a little scamp much of the time, it was rare for her to see such an easy smile on Peggy, so she accepted it readily. "He was a horror as a baby, really. My father was the only one who could calm him."

"Not your mother?" asked Peggy, seeming to be the one who was nervous.

Sometimes, any question about someone who had died

made people uneasy, Judith had noticed. She had wanted to shout at her father's parishioners, and sometimes, she did snap at them. They had no need to avoid mentioning her mother, to avoid visiting, or to talk in low tones. *What did they imagine the family did all day when they could think of nothing else?* Just one normal conversation with someone outside their house would have been enough to set them up, but there were few. Only others who had been bereaved could speak to them, and their straightforward kindness made Judith ashamed for how she had once avoided them after their own losses.

Judith's grief was long and bitter. Sometimes, she felt that her father had moved the whole family what felt like a continent away, even if it was only a few days' journey, to keep her from making sharp and shameful remarks to members of his flock.

"My mother, when he was hungry," said Judith, looking at the baby. "But the rest of the time, it was my father. Pacing but with just the right rhythm. I thought I got it a few times, but Joseph never liked it as much when it was not my father."

The leaves were still, and Judith looked over at the Lambs' again. It was amazing how adding to the dimensions of the solid house had raised its capacity quite a bit. A dozen people were staying there apart from the Lambs, and the infant would be another—if she could survive.

"Mothers' milk is better for her than cow's milk," said Judith. "Surely we could get a wet nurse out for her."

Peggy looked rather shocked. "I thought some spoke against having a wet nurse."

"That French gentleman, perhaps. I forget his name. But my mother always said it would be lunacy to keep a child from its best food simply to uphold those ideals. A wet nurse ought to be the second step, though, not the first. That's what she said, anyway."

When she got no response, Judith flushed. "Well, not lunacy. I mean, I do not think my mother used the word lunacy—"

"Calm yourself, Judith. I have only been thinking of the cost. I said something to Margaret, and she said that the subscribers would not wish funds to be used in that way."

"They would have us take her to a foundling hospital, then? Where if she did not die, she would not know love or kindness?"

Peggy's eyes flashed. "I am sure I know more of foundling hospitals than you do. And I would never allow her to be taken to such a place."

Judith had forgotten. No matter how much she learned about her friend's life, she would always think of Peggy as one of the Haddingtons, a family so rich they could have belonged to a castle in a fairy tale.

Peggy had leaned closer to the baby and was kissing her brow. "We will see you safe," she murmured without looking at Judith.

"I'm sorry." Judith cursed herself for the blunders she kept making with everyone around her.

"Stop troubling yourself, Judith. I can take care of myself well enough and look out for this child as well."

Her response was pointed, and Judith found herself looking down at her fingertips. "Do you wish to speak about your husband?"

Peggy stroked the child's downy head. "No," she said, then she put her thumb in the child's small fist. "Or perhaps. I wish I knew."

**10**

---

The park could not have been more beautiful, though it was still near enough to the bustle of the city that it would never be mistaken for countryside. Still, the sense of being a mite closer to nature offered Louisa-Margaretta precious moments away from her social obligations. She strode about, her limbs humming with energy. She could never walk slowly enough to suit Federica, which her friend noticed instantly.

"You should have found someone else," she scolded her, touching her belly as she lagged behind Louisa-Margaretta. "I am only going to get slower."

"I should have found someone who would not let me speak with anyone we encountered, gentleman or lady."

"It would be too obvious if I gave in to your wish to avoid everyone, Louie."

"Why would you make such an accusation?"

"This is the second time you have dragged me behind a tree. I am not quite in a fit state for hiding, and I am sure that everyone can still see me. I look like a boulder."

Perhaps Federica had exaggerated, but Louisa-

Margaretta had adeptly steered her friend off the path. By that point, she had lived in London enough to know friends, foes, and bores. And she had made precious few friends.

"My mind is idle," she said. "And for that reason, I cannot be forced into even a few minutes of idle conversation. It would drive me mad."

"You're not likely to find much else here." Federica leaned heavily against the tree in a most unladylike manner. "Besides, if your mind is idle, nobody is keeping you from the libraries or the museums."

Louisa-Margaretta felt as if she were sinking when she thought of museums. Certain paintings had such intensity of color and imagination that they left her transported in a way that few books ever seemed to accomplish. And the curiosities were reminders that, even if she had never left England, she might someday dream of her own grand tour. But since her last trip to a museum had ended in heartbreak, she was determined never to strut about galleries again. If she had to live all her days avoiding the paintings that had stood proudly by as she gave away her heart and made a fool of herself, she would be ignorant, but at least she might save herself some measure of pain.

"I do not wish to read," Louisa-Margaretta said haughtily. "I want to ride, shoot, and explore. I want to join the army and go kill Napoleon Bonaparte."

"You would be rather something as a general." Federica smiled, but it was wistful. She was not laughing. In fact, she appeared transported by a serious vision of her friend commanding a sea of troops. "I would love to see you as a sort of modern Joan of Arc."

Louisa-Margaretta gave a curt nod. "Exactly. All these years later, you would think they have learned nothing. A woman cannot shoot, she cannot ride, and she cannot lead armies."

"Well, a lady cannot. How well do you like being a lady?"

Louisa-Margaretta frowned, unable to miss the tartness in Federica's voice. Her friend, though of the same class, did not have the luxury of limitless funds or a great deal of money that was settled on her alone. Louisa-Margaretta was not blind to the more mercenary reasons that had nudged Federica into marrying young.

"It does not signify whether I like it," Louisa-Margaretta said. "I am a lady. That is all."

When she thought of giving up her fine clothing and large homes, the prospect did not fill her with dread. It was simply unthinkable, like a bird deciding to live underground or a horse choosing to live in a tree.

"You are a very elegant lady" came a voice at her shoulder, "and you are to be accorded all due respect."

Federica acknowledged him with some trepidation though notably without actual fear. "Mr Fortescue, you are looking well."

He gave her a muted smile. "Mrs Gillingham, you are too kind. Are you quite well yourself?"

"Well, I am feeling rather faint. I believe I will take advantage of the patch of shade just there to rest."

She moved slowly, looking back at Louisa-Margaretta as if she expected her to follow. Nobody could have accused her of completely neglecting her duties as a chaperone, though she did not issue any commands.

Louisa-Margaretta, though she had every excuse to get away from the interloper, found that she did no more than step back a couple of paces. He had gotten closer to her than was strictly becoming in a gentleman.

"Miss Haddington, I believe I have interrupted a rather fascinating conversation."

Louisa-Margaretta paused, trying not to look directly at the man. She was not impressed by his accent or his manners. His looks, however, were another matter, and she found that it was safest to avoid confronting those directly.

"My dreams of killing Napoleon Bonaparte are colorful," she said. "But I do not know that I would find them fascinating. In spite of my friend's best wishes, I shall never be a general, so I daresay I need take no particular pains over my strategy."

"Do tell me of your dreams."

"Why bother? You do not care for my dreams, and neither does anyone in the ton. You may as well ask about my fortune, my prospects, or perhaps even the scandals in my family. That is all anyone really wishes to know."

"You have a very low opinion of me, then."

"My opinion of you is the common one," she insisted. "But I am the only lady in this city willing to speak it aloud."

That did not amuse him.

"I might ask why ladies have low opinions of me yet will say nothing to me directly. That is, if the feelings are as universal as you claim."

She could see that her laughter needled him. "Oh, please listen to yourself, Mr Fortescue, if you do not listen to me. One can hardly go around toying with both the feelings and reputations of young ladies as well as drinking with England's most famous rakes without expecting to acquire some sort of reputation. Even the freedom you are granted as a young, rich, exotic man cannot hope to fully protect you there."

Before he could respond, a thundering of hooves sounded, and they both turned to look.

A phaeton was being driven through the park much too fast. In some places, one could gallop, of course, but a path already full of languid ladies strolling about with parasols was hardly one of them. Louisa-Margaretta nearly went to Federica to make sure that she, in her condition, had not been shocked and realised even she was breathing quickly and loudly.

Mr Fortescue, on the other hand, seemed completely undisturbed. He noticed her disquiet and appeared to consider it a victory. When Louisa-Margaretta caught her breath, wondering how such a spindly horse could have frightened her, he quoted: "The earthquake came and rocked the quivering wall, and men and nature reeled as if with wine. Whom did I seek around the tottering hall? For thee. Whose safety first provide for? Thine."

She raised an eyebrow at him. "Lord Byron? How dull."

Mr Fortescue scoffed. "I can assure you his company is anything but dull."

"I am sure I would find it so. His poetry is little more than one of the cheapest novels, tarted up with a bit of rhyme."

She could not tell whether his incredulity came from her assertion that Byron's poetry was unworthy or from her use of the word "tarted" in her description. She decided he might find both equally shocking.

"And whose poetry do you prefer, then, if you reject what is both popular and praised in literary circles?"

"I prefer Goethe's work if I must read poetry. I can assure you it is not a favorite pastime of mine, but occasionally, one of my brothers forces me to listen."

"Your German is up to the task, then?"

"I never worked hard at it, much to my governess's despair, but I have a good-enough memory. It is more than enough for me to be able to tell that his style is far superior to Byron's, as is his subject matter."

He gave a ghost of a smile. "Well, I cannot agree with you. But perhaps I have found Lord Byron to be such a worthy companion that I have overlooked any flaws in his poetry."

"If by 'worthy,' you mean 'infamous,' yes, you would be correct there."

"I never thought you were one for moralizing, Miss Haddington."

"Oh, I assure you all morals bore me nearly as much as those who delight in enforcing them. But I find Lord Byron's idea of fun rather dull. Anyone can put on a colorful head-dress and drink wine, perhaps while encouraging others to do the same. I would die of boredom."

"You would rather be in a factory, then? Or perhaps in the countryside, in some quaint little shooting party?"

Louisa-Margaretta could not be surprised that he knew her family. In fact, he had probably heard more than she might wish about the house her parents had bought in the country and even perhaps its purpose. If he imagined she had felt trapped in that large home, hidden away from one particularly ineligible gentleman and likely doomed into marriage with some odious country neighbour, he would be correct. She had longed for escape, and still, she longed never to go back to Derbyshire without the freedom that marriage would afford her.

But he could not have known how much she had loved the countryside, how the cold of the North had taken hold of her soul in a romance that was worthy of poetry.

"I like riding," she said, "and I like shooting. Nothing that I enjoy is quaint, which is the problem with the ton. Everything here is dull."

She allowed herself to look at him, noticing again that his face seemed nearly perfect in its beauty, and cast her eyes down. "Exceedingly dull."

"Do you wish to travel the world?"

"Why? Do you have a ship to sell me?"

He laughed at her, his annoyance past. "No, but you could come as my wife."

"I would not trust you to be a devoted husband. I am not going to be like the poor wife of the Prince of Wales. If one's husband is worse than any bachelor, the marriage vows are a public joke, and the whole thing is not worth the trouble."

"A proposal and a rejection in the same afternoon! My, but this is a day of firsts."

"It does not surprise me that you have not proposed to a young woman. You enjoy their favors and attentions, never thinking of them as human beings."

"I could never marry someone who agreed with all my opinions, which so far seems to be the pattern I have observed in every unmarried young lady of fashion."

"You mean only that they do not express their disagreement. Your opinions are so ill-founded that I am sure more than one unmarried young lady does not agree with a single one of them."

"And your opinions are fascinating if misinformed. I cannot agree with your rejection of me, for example."

Again, she tried not to look at him. Surely she would hate everything about becoming that man's wife. Everything, perhaps, except those mysteries Federica refused to fully explain. Even though Louisa-Margaretta was familiar with classical texts and the more scandalous modern ones, a great deal about marriage was still left to her imagination. The wife of Mr Fortescue was likely to find some very great enjoyment. Though she would pay dearly for that.

"Well," she said, "I hope you will not meet with rejection again."

His ill temper was back. "One might wonder, if you would turn down such a proposal as this, who on earth could hope to tempt you."

She resisted telling him the truth. He did not deserve to know the extent to which she had once loved and still stupidly wished to devote herself to another. At least her parents and Isaac's had done such a thorough job of hiding the truth that many of their set did not know.

"Someone who would wish to marry only me," she said. "A suitor who would accept no substitute."

For a moment, he stayed silent, and she was able to listen to the wind in the trees around them. She wondered how he had managed to waste time drinking with the country's most famous romantic poet without having the least notion of chivalry or devotion. It only confirmed her opinion that George III, Lord Byron, and most gentlemen of her acquaintance were blathering idiots. She wondered how on earth she would ever manage to tolerate London for the length of time it would take to find one she could stand to marry.

"I must be going," she said with a curtsy so small that the insult was plain. "It has been a pleasure."

And as she walked with her friend, she realised that it had been.

With Mr Fortescue, at least, she had not needed idle talk. For one afternoon, she had been permitted to speak plainly, and she felt freer for it.

**11**

---

Judith had left the room to give Mercy and the doctor some privacy. The weekly visits were supposed to be examinations of Mercy's form and health, but Judith could not help but note that they had become less and less frequent in recent months. When Margaret reminded the doctor of that the day before, his face had grown unfriendly.

"I have not forgotten her," he said with such vehemence that Judith was sure he had.

"I would never make such an accusation," said Margaret, "nor would I say that our Mercy wants for anything."

"I hope not," ventured Judith. "But I would be more than happy to help, of course, if there is something else thou wouldst wish me to do."

Her offer petered away when she saw the expression of distaste on the doctor's face and the disappointment on Margaret's.

Judith was under no illusions about her skills. They were modest enough. If she did something well, it was because she had tried it in the past and got a good result.

She did not have the instincts that would have helped her. She had not Peggy's gentle ease, Bathsheba's unfettered laughter, or Margaret's quiet authority. All she had were her memories, learning on her feet, and her determination to see Peggy well. Since Peggy had healed, at least to some degree, she would have liked to see Mercy well too. But apparently, she was not even successful at keeping Mercy calm.

"Mercy does very well in Judith's care," said Margaret a bit too slowly. She was not the sort of person to criticise in a deceptive manner. If she was unhappy, surely, she would have told Judith.

"I will see her tomorrow," the doctor insisted.

"We will be here for luncheon," Judith explained rather hastily. "Perhaps you could see her then."

"You are here for luncheon more and more," said the doctor. So he had noticed, then. He was using "you" to refer to both Judith and Mercy.

"The pace seems to suit her. Things are never hasty at the Lambs' table."

"They may become a bit hastier if my husband will keep ordering Bathsheba into the kitchen," said Margaret with the ghost of a smile. "I have told him that surely wasting food is a greater sin than allowing her a respite from the cooking."

"She should have a respite from everything if she needs it," said the doctor. "Not just the cooking."

"It is best that she occupy her mind," insisted Margaret. "She is in my care and need not be shut off from the world."

In the moment of silence, Mercy went to the window. Judith nearly stomped her foot in frustration. Though she could never be quite sure how much Mercy understood, she realised they had all broken Margaret's policy of not speaking of anyone who was in the room. If anyone was cut off from the world, it was Mercy, and Judith hoped that Margaret's strange observation about Bathsheba had not caused Mercy any heartache.

"We will see you for lunch tomorrow," Judith promised, though she dreaded the idea of having to sit through the whole meal with the doctor. When she was with ladies, it was much easier to tolerate the occasional dark or chiding contribution from Jacob Lamb. But when the doctor was there, the tenor of the table changed, and somehow, the men cast a greater shadow. Mercy never seemed quite so easy, either, though Judith would never have said so to anyone besides Peggy.

In the morning, Judith was careful to explain to Mercy why they would be eating with the Lambs, and during their noon respite, they walked across the green to eat a modest meal before the examination. The lunch itself went better than Judith had expected. The doctor was delayed because of William, another guest, and he sent word that the whole party should start without him. As it turned out, they ended up finishing the meal without him, and Judith was just on the verge of walking back across the lawn with Mercy when he came in.

During the examination, Judith felt uneasy. With another person, she might have asked to stay in the room, but it was different with Mercy and the doctor. And she could hardly be seen pacing outside the door—it would look as if she were trying to listen at the keyhole.

A squalling came from upstairs, followed by silence, and she asked Margaret if she could go see the baby. She had nearly forgotten about the tiny thing.

Margaret nodded, but she looked troubled. "Let me go up first. I will come back down for thee."

After several minutes, she returned. "They are ready for thee. The baby is sleeping."

When Judith walked into one of the upstairs bedrooms, which she supposed had become a nursery of sorts, she saw a woman she vaguely recognised from the village.

"This is Joyce Garvey," said Margaret. "Thanks to you and to our Peggy, she will be with us to care for the child for some time. This is Judith St Clair, my right hand."

Judith blushed at the praise. Joyce ran a practiced eye down her. "Miss St Clair, is it, then?"

"Judith," she said and noticed the woman's skeptical eye. "But yes, I am not married."

"Not from around here either," said the woman. "Though not far."

"I grew up in Essex. But my father moved us to Derbyshire when he found a new patron some years ago."

"I understand," said Joyce.

Judith looked down. She felt that the wet nurse was the kind of woman who learned all sorts of information without ever seeming to gossip and wondered if the fact that Judith's father enjoyed the patronage of Peggy's mother-in-law had already reached the woman's ears. Peggy, a young woman with wealthy connections, choosing to stay on in such an establishment was not unusual. For Judith, who was neither a Quaker nor a former "guest" of the home, it must seem rather queer from the outside, especially since Judith was still a rector's daughter and had not abandoned her faith.

Suddenly, she recognised Joyce from the little church in the village and asked her if she attended regularly.

"Not every Sunday, dear, no. I'm thankful for what I have, but sometimes, the worry keeps me away just as sure as it draws me in."

Margaret straightened. "There are many paths to God, to be sure."

"Yes, but we've got to eat. This last winter, it was too long for all of us."

"Indeed," said Judith. "I remember." And she did, though she realised with a pang that she had mostly been thinking of the people in her orbit and their need for fresh air and green gardens, not the more pressing need for food. When the home's stores were low, they were always able to get it in from somewhere, and she never even had to be troubled about the accounts the way she would have been had she stayed in her father's house.

"And the year before that, a poor harvest," the woman went on, tucking the swaddling clothes round the baby with a practiced hand. "Remember, then, how the winter before, the Thames froze? Just ice, all it was. People coming from London and all sorts. I thought they were telling tales, but no, we heard it even from the likes of my niece, who has never been one for tall tales."

"I am so sorry," said Judith. "I did not realise."

"Best not to think of such things," said Joyce firmly. "We all survived it. That's true enough. There, she's stirring. You'd like to hold her?"

"Won't she mind?"

"Mind? She's a baby. She would like nothing better."

## 12

—————

Judith had not wanted to take the infant into her arms, but holding her, she did feel calmer in an instant. It had never quite been like that with her brothers. She was always afraid she would drop them or at least hold them awkwardly so their heads lolled back. In the chair, with that child, she did not feel anything of the sort. For the first time, she had a sense of the peace her mother must have felt. Judith had always seen her squalling brothers as a burden, each one a strange creature that must be cared for until it could at least move about on its own. But finally, she felt the charm.

And the baby herself must have known those feelings, because she quieted and looked up at Judith, her little hands feeling about until at last, Judith offered one of her fingers, and the baby took it. It was the action of any baby, but she smiled in spite of herself.

She was so absorbed in the baby's soft, delicate face that she hardly noticed Margaret leaving or Joyce opening and closing drawers.

"What are you doing with the child?" came a voice from the doorway, and Judith started.

Joyce frowned, shaking her head. "You must keep your voice lower, sir. You'll startle her."

And indeed, the baby had started to fuss, though as Judith moved, she quieted again.

"This infant is not thy charge, Judith," said the doctor.

Judith frowned. "I know who my charge is, and she was otherwise occupied. Have you left her all alone?"

She did not wish to use "thou" with the doctor. Sometimes, she wished for the cold formality that "you" afforded, particularly when he treated her with disrespect.

He moved to take the child, but Judith put her soundly back in the nurse's arms, saying she might still be hungry.

"Mercy is waiting," he said.

"And how is she?" Judith asked, challenging him. She did not know how much Joyce had been told, but even though the woman's hands were busy arranging the infant at her breast, her eyes were fixed on the doctor.

"She is well, if a little tan. Thou must see to it that she wears her bonnet."

"She has done much better with a parasol for some time, if it is a fashionable one. She never wears a bonnet for anyone here."

Judith knew the doctor would feel the reproof. She could not even say why he was still in the room if not simply to scold her.

"I will speak to Margaret Lamb, then," he said. "I had no idea she was being neglected."

Judith stared at him then rushed from the room.

Fortunately, Margaret was the one sitting with Mercy in the room the doctor had abandoned. He had likely gone without even saying a proper goodbye to the poor woman.

Mercy was toying with some yarn. Apparently, when she was well, she had never much enjoyed a workbasket. But now, she liked to fiddle with the materials, almost as a cat would or a child still too young to ply a needle.

Judith, who could cope with fits, screams, and broken china, was in tears after the doctor's scolding It was not only the coldness of his words. He was happy to make demands on her and mistrust her at the same time.

"Judith," said Margaret, leading her to a chair. She did not tell Judith not to cry or that all would be well, which Judith appreciated. Sometimes, the expertise that people developed living with those who were deemed mad was necessary even for more ordinary quarrels.

"The doctor said I have been neglecting Mercy," Judith managed, whispering through her tears. She did not want Mercy to hear, but she needed to tell Margaret her story before the doctor got to her.

"I am sure that cannot be true. I have seen thy constant care and attention. Our friend has done extraordinarily well with you."

That made Judith cry more, for Mercy was not well. She was far from cured. It was certainly true that, with Judith, she had mostly refrained from the behaviors that had made everyone think it necessary for her to have a caregiver dedicated solely to her. But still, she could not speak, there were many things she did not appear to understand, and were she to venture into the outside world, it was certain that idiocy or madness or some other terrible word would be applied to her.

"He does not even see her every day," said Judith, still whispering. "He is free to see other patients or to see nobody. Or to walk in the woods, as he often used to. Though, he does not do so very often now."

Margaret stiffened. She removed the bunch of yarn Mercy had started to reach for and replaced it with another color, though Judith could not think why.

"Perhaps the doctor is troubled," Margaret managed. "But I am very sure he should not have said such things to thee. And his charges of neglect reflect only his mind, not anything of substance, as a still pond may reflect the sky and the clouds without showing the colour of the water."

Margaret said the phrase to anyone who was newly arrived. Judith remembered how, at first, it had been nearly impossible not to feel scared or hurt by the words and actions of some of the people around her. Only once she understood the depth of their pain and saw them recover from some of these behaviors was she able to feel less scared.

But for the doctor, it did not quite seem right. Perhaps it was his position of authority. Judith felt he should have known not to speak to her in that manner, especially since she was with Mercy most of the hours of the day and was in a position to exact revenge through neglect. *I would never consider that course, but if I did, who would realise it?*

Judith heard the baby crying in the next room, which only unsettled her more. The low tones of the doctor came again. *Why,* she wondered, *does he insist on staying there with the infant, bothering the poor wet nurse, who is a stranger to our ways?* It was as if he wanted an infant for an easy patient. He was always trying to hold and examine the babe, saying she might have been abandoned because she was ill. That, to Judith, seemed blind as well as stupid. Anyone could see that the little one was perfectly healthy, and the doctor was truly ignorant if he did not understand the crippling cost of trying to feed a family after a poor harvest.

"He walks out with great freedom," she could not help

saying. "And I run about after Mercy, but he thinks nothing of that."

She knew she should not have repeated it. Margaret was plainly not fond of hearing about the doctor's walks, though she turned toward Judith.

"My dear," she said, "thy mind will be much easier with some sort of excursion. Indeed, I know we are not very cheerful company here, especially at the moment. Tomorrow, I will care for Mercy, and we will see that a half day is given to thee. But do try to leave, if that is possible. It is better for the mind to get free of the site of all the troubles."

Judith felt a flush of shame. Margaret Lamb, as the female superintendent and one of the people most worried over the little infant in their midst, could least afford to spare the time.

"I should not," she said. "I thank thee for such kindness, but truly, I could not possibly accept it."

"Nonsense," said the woman brusquely, patting Mercy's shoulder. Once again, both of them had been guilty of forgetting about Mercy in all the turmoil. "I will enjoy spending time with Mercy. Mercy, I shall call for thee tomorrow just before breakfast, and after luncheon, thou wilt be with our Judith."

Judith escorted Mercy from the house, and as they walked across the lawn, she noticed that her charge seemed different—perhaps sad or maybe only weary. The walk was a slow one.

*Tomorrow,* she thought. *Tomorrow, I shall walk out on my own, and perhaps some of the sorrow will lift.*

Her heart and her throat still felt heavy, even as they left the small building to return to the larger one. She fancied she could feel the doctor's dark spirit descending on both of them.

**13**

———

The morning dawned clear. As breakfast approached, Judith thought she ought to be jubilant. She had a half day to spend as she wished, with no more command than to leave the property, the one thing she most wished to do. If it had rained or even been muddy, she might have felt trapped.

The problem was as she walked away, she still felt trapped. In fact, it was almost a worse morning, as she kept wondering about Mercy.

Mercy had been uncommonly placid. She had not woken early or dragged Judith out into the garden. In fact, she had not made any trouble.

Although Judith could not say for certain that Mercy had not woken early. When she herself stirred, realizing that it was later than the usual hour, Mercy's eyes were wide open and filled with tears. She was crying, the tears soaking her pillow, but she made no move to wipe them away.

"Mercy," said Judith, chilly as she went over to the other bed without bothering with a housecoat. "Mercy, whatever's the matter?"

Mercy did not fight, but neither did she smile all morning. She wore the pale face of a mourner.

"It must be grief," said Judith when Margaret arrived. They were standing in the hall, the door open just enough for Judith to hear if something went wrong. "She looks just as if she has lost someone very dear to her."

Margaret usually did not dismiss any of Judith's theories, but she shook her head. "I'm sure that is not it, dear. For whom could she have lost? Mercy lives here, and nobody has left in some time."

"Apart from Bathsheba."

"But Bathsheba has returned," snapped the older woman, opening the door and gazing at Mercy, who was lying on the bed, fully dressed.

"Yes, but perhaps, seeing as she was such a fixture here, the long absence?"

"Bathsheba has nothing to do with it," said Margaret a bit more calmly, pushing the door until it was nearly closed again.

"I know this is grief," persisted Judith, though it was unlike her to argue. "It is something beyond words, and I have seen it. I have lived it."

Since the day before, Judith had been rather lifeless herself, angry at the doctor and at the superintendent, who had a talent for making work that should have been sacred into something bitter and thankless.

But she recovered some of her spirits in defending Mercy. It was more than the poor woman just absorbing Judith's black mood. She was living through some loss of her own.

"It may be a memory," said Margaret more gently.

"Could it have been something the doctor said to her? Or something she did?"

"Do not blame the doctor for this. What he said to thee was unkind, but he cannot have put Mercy in such a state. I will take her down to breakfast. That may help revive her."

Judith knew it would not. But she also knew a dismissal when she heard one. So she had taken a bit of money, in case she found something to buy in the village, and her best coat along with some bread and cheese from the kitchen. And she had gone on her way with a troubled heart, wondering why she had been thrust into the position of Mercy's sole defender.

*Peggy might hear me out,* she reflected. She had been less out of temper with Judith ever since the foundling appeared. Whenever Peggy was near the child, her face was softer, her spirit calmer. Judith had noticed similar in herself, only much more so, and it forced her to remember how much Peggy had once longed for a child. In fact, that had been one of the many things that had brought on her madness, the knowledge that her husband would not help her adopt an infant. It was not her fault that she could not give birth to a little Haddington, but Percival had not been moved.

Judith was so out of temper when she remembered that provocation that she entered the tiny village in ill humour. Though the walk had been brisk and beautiful, and she should have taken comfort in some little trinket or other, she was even more out of spirits.

*What? Shall I ever sigh and pine?* she thought, but she could get no wisdom from the old poem. It seemed that whether she stayed or left, unhappiness was bound to follow her, and she had to either cede ground to a life of suffering or continue fighting the men who disregarded her opinion.

She felt still worse when she encountered Percival

himself, standing in one of the little village shops. He started then smiled, following her out.

"Miss Haddington," he said, "please forgive me. I am very glad to see you again."

She did not wish to speak with him but could not ignore him in public. It would set the whole village gossiping, and the Lambs would likely wonder whether she was ever fit to be out in the world again.

"I hope you have concluded your business here in the village, Mr Haddington," she said. "And I hope that your family is well."

"My parents could be worse," he said. "Father is busy enough in Manchester now that he has no reason to stay in the country and fail to influence his wayward daughter. Mama is concerning herself in everyone's business, and she may be making herself into a bit of a nuisance, I'm afraid."

Judith stopped walking, staring at the man. "The entire village is thankful for your mother's attention," she said. "Many would be considerably worse off if not for her kindness."

Judith did not like to put herself in that same category, but the plain truth was that the patrons of any living often had an outsize influence on the life of the person who was fortunate enough to claim it, not to mention the future of that person's family. Judith knew quite well that her father was fortunate to have a patron who was both kind and religious, particularly after so many years of living in poverty. He was deserving, to be sure, but that did not mean he would be treated justly wherever he went.

"I know my mother's generosity, and I know her propensity for meddling," he said. "But since you can be so kind to her, perhaps you could extend some of that forgiveness to me and allow me to speak to you of my wife."

Judith sighed. "Your wife is dear to me." She hesitated. "But she is more than capable of making her own decisions. If she wishes to stay at the home, I cannot convince her otherwise."

"Oh, she is quite ready to leave," said Mr Haddington. "I gleaned as much the other day. Only, she does not wish to come back to me or to the scoundrels I hesitate to call her birth family, and that leaves her with rather little."

"Her life here is full enough. Especially now that the child has come, she seems quite content with it."

She was not telling the truth. Peggy, as she became well, had become less content. Though she was taken with the infant, on the whole, she was less than happy.

"Will you do nothing to help me? My wife has not forgiven me, and my sister is acting even more rashly than I would have believed. She is truly putting herself in danger."

"Louisa-Margaretta told me she would never be in very great danger because she is such an excellent shot."

"She said something similar the last time I saw her."

Judith laughed.

"I do not find it the least bit funny," he continued. "Louisa-Margaretta has no sense of what she has to lose. Even my parents, though they indulged her for quite a long time, are not going to forgive any misstep. They would turn her out if she were to truly offend them."

Judith considered that. "And if they did turn her out?"

He looked shocked. "What?"

"If they did turn her out," said Judith, "she would have to work. And I am sure she is quite capable."

He frowned. "Louisa-Margaretta, working for wages? A lady of quality?"

"I think there is nothing wanting about myself in terms of quality," said Judith. "And I earn wages for the work I do.

What is more, the work itself is important, as you have seen. Even your wife earns a wage now, though you may be loath to admit it."

He swallowed. "That is quite different. And of course, we mean to contribute all those funds to the place where she has stayed. That she wishes to help others at this home, well, this is what many grand ladies do, is it not?"

"Ladies swan in and out of these places as they please. They come for a Sunday lunch or for an afternoon when they have no other fixed engagement. They do not watch over dozens of women, keeping them safe, bathing them, and feeding them when they cannot feed themselves."

Percival recoiled, but she continued. "It is ugly work at times, and sometimes, even the families of those we help hate us because we are doing what they cannot accomplish or cannot bear to attempt. And they treat us worse than most gentlemen can imagine."

She softened her face. "Though, I am sure you can imagine it. You have been ill-treated yourself."

"And still you will not help me," he said. "Not even if it meant you could leave here?"

Judith gave a bitter laugh. "Why would I leave? I have nowhere for me to go. Back to my father's house, where my sister hates me and I would hear village gossip on every visit, every day of the week? Or perhaps I could marry. I have noted well how such a thing works for many young women who choose it."

"That is not a kind thing to say of marriage."

"All the women who come to us are married."

Strictly speaking, that was not true. *Nearly* all the women who came to them were married. But Judith noted few differences between the two groups, and unlike Percival, most of the husbands seemed more than happy to stay away until their wives were eventually sent back home.

"So you leave my sister to me," he said slowly. "Even knowing that she may find her way to a very unfortunate match or worse."

Judith shuddered a bit at the implications. If Louisa-Margaretta were diving headfirst into a true scandal, she ought to rescue her.

Yet she was so very tired. The doctor's words, Mercy's tears, and the harsh glare of the superintendent as he stared at the infant who had upended everything—the place that had made her believe herself capable, a worthy being beyond her status as a rector's daughter and a gentlewoman, was fast accomplishing the opposite.

"You are her brother," she said. "I trust you to take care of her."

But as Judith returned to the home, she wondered whether she had misplaced her trust. For even across many silent months and miles, she felt that something must be amiss with Louisa-Margaretta.

**14**

―――

Federica smiled when they stepped into the assembly room.

"I thought you said you were tired." Louisa-Margaretta grinned at her. "Yet we come here, and it is as if a wilting flower has begun to bloom again."

"I always hated this place before I was married," said Federica dreamily. "But now, when I do not have to worry about that sort of thing, it is great fun."

"I'm sure it must be," said Louisa-Margaretta, pouting.

"Oh, Louie, your time will come."

"You cannot promise I will find a suitor who is worthy, surely. I could come here for years more and still hate every gentleman I meet."

"Yes, but if you return for years, you will be able to see the place with a sort of detached amusement, as I do. And unless I am much mistaken, you have not hated *every* gentleman."

Louisa-Margaretta tried not to blush. She had decided to avoid Mr Fortescue. Until she met him, it had been easy for her to reject gentlemen she considered unworthy. After all, since each of them had quickly moved on to another young lady, they had proven that their interest in her was quite fleeting.

And Mr Fortescue, of all of them, was the most likely to move on. It seemed he would always be seeking other pleasures, and if he was anything like Lord Byron, he likely did not care whether he married.

Louisa-Margaretta should have been able to forget him, but she could not. She had lied to her friend when she said that she wanted to go to the assembly rooms simply as a way for the two of them to leave the confines of Federica's small but comfortable home. In fact, she had heard a rumor that Mr Fortescue would be there. Though she did not mean to dance with him, his presence attracted her. If he asked her, she had decided, she would say that she was indisposed and refuse to dance with anyone at all, so as not to give offense. And she would have to watch him dancing with every pretty girl or desperate pauper who was pushed into his path. But the thought of him drew her, and she could not resist it.

"It will, perhaps, be more enjoyable if I do despise every gentleman," said Louisa-Margaretta with a sniff. "But I will not accept any of them until I find someone who deserves me."

"And if the season ends without you finding anyone? What will you do then? Go back to the country home you swore to escape? For you are no general, and there is no other path open to you," said Federica.

Only, it wasn't Federica. She had turned to greet another married friend who had also come to the assembly rooms as a chaperone. Federica had spoken only in Louisa-Margaretta's imagination. She would never have said something so callous, only Louisa-Margaretta knew that the harsh truth was the right one. Unless she took a path that was very rocky or married soon, Federica's confinement would begin. With a new baby, Federica would be unable to act a chaperone, and Louisa-Margaretta would be forced out. She would have no choice but to either return to her parents or live under the rule of one of her brothers, which would certainly be worse.

As if to emphasise that fact, one of them appeared before her.

"Percival," Louisa-Margaretta said with a rather cold smile. "I wonder that you always seek me out here, when you know you are always welcome in my friend's home."

"I do not see your friend," he said. "It seems that you are here almost entirely on her own."

"Don't be tiresome. She is not three yards from us, talking with Mrs Walters, who is her particular friend. I cannot help it that she has other friends. She is so agreeable."

"Perhaps you might learn from her."

Louisa-Margaretta laughed. "Oh, dear Percival, I am always agreeable. Just because I am quarreling with Mama and Papa does not mean I have changed in that respect."

"You have certainly changed, for the world at large never thought you agreeable before."

"I thought you did, darling."

Percival had always been Louisa-Margaretta's favorite, and he certainly adored her as well. Even after he had gone into the army, she often sought his company. Only after all the trouble with Peggy did the two of them fall out, and even now, she would have warmed to him—would have, had he not sought to control her.

"You must leave this life," he said. "It is not for you, and you have no idea how dangerous some of the men can be."

"Don't worry, Percival. It is no longer the fashion to carry swords about. There was some doddering old fool of at least ninety who tried it last week, but even unarmed, I would have been more than a match for him."

"I know that Mr Fortescue has been continuing to pay you every attention. I hear you have quite caught his fancy."

Louisa-Margaretta tried not to betray the pleasure she felt on hearing this statement. "I am sure some new young woman catches his fancy every week, and I cannot help if I happen to be one of them. I assure you I have done nothing to encourage him."

"He has not called on you?"

"No, and I am sure he would not. I should not be at home, at any rate."

Percival let out a breath. "Well, that is something," he managed. "Because if you were ever seen with him, if there were even a hint of a rumor—"

"Darling Percival, there have been many rumors surrounding our family, and some of the worst ones have turned out to be true. I hardly think this could do the Haddington name any more damage."

His pale skin flushed. "As I said, you have very little idea of the damage it could do, not just to our family but to you in particular. And that is why I am asking you to come to the country with me."

"Unless you are going to throw me over your shoulder and bundle me into a carriage waiting outside the door, I believe I can safely promise you never to go back to the country."

"I am thinking of you."

"And I am thinking of myself. So we are well matched there. Thank you for your concern for my reputation, but I can assure you I am more than able to guard it myself."

After the briefest of pauses, Percival tried a different tack. "I need your help with Peggy."

"I have already refused," she said. "What makes you think asking in the same way, in the same place, is going to do you any favors? She is your wife, so you must help yourself."

"I need your help with Judith."

She could not help finally looking at him, peering closely into his eyes. "Judith has been helping Peggy, and from everything I hear, she loved that awful madhouse place so well that she decided to stay there forever and adopt some strange Quaker customs. Her father will not like it, perhaps, but what have I to do with her decision?"

"Judith is unhappy," said Percival. "She does not wish to stay, but she feels she cannot abandon Peggy there or some other woman that she was going on about."

"That is still her decision."

"She feels she has nowhere else to go."

That made Louisa-Margaretta pause. Though she felt for Peggy, she was more or less happy to refuse. And even the mention of Judith might not have been enough to sway her. But the mention of Judith's cage shook her. Louisa-Margaretta, for all her wealth and beauty, was in much the same situation as Judith, the young woman who had once been her closest friend—unable to stand the life she was living, unable to contemplate changing to one that was even more staid and confining.

"And you think I am the only one who can help her?"

At that moment, Percival could have swayed her. He could have seized his advantage, reaching for the tender feelings his sister still harbored for someone she must always consider a friend, in spite of the many months of coldness that had passed between them.

Instead, he turned away. "I am not sure she deserves help," he said with some bitterness. "She means to keep me from Peggy, and you are the only way to get past her."

"So I'm a key for a lock, am I?"

His face fell. "Well, no."

Louisa-Margaretta was rescued once again by the very man her brother had ostensibly come to warn her about.

"Mr Fortescue," she said with warmth. "What a pleasure to see you."

"An unusually kind reception," he responded with a raise of his eyebrows. "You've put your sister in better humor, eh, Haddington?"

Percival moved as if to strike him, but Louisa-Margaretta held his arm with a silky smile.

"What wonderful musicians," she said despite that the orchestra had been uncommonly out of tune all evening.

Mr Fortescue did not need prodding in order to accept the hint. It would have been unseemly for a young woman to ask him to dance directly, but he wasted no time asking Louisa-Margaretta.

And she wasted no time in accepting.

The look on Percival's face as she walked away with a prize "dangerous" man was nearly as thrilling to her as the drop in her heart when Mr Fortescue held her rather closer than the dance required.

---

## 15

Judith spent most of the walk back trying to have a good cry.

*Would it not be better to cry, as I did the other day, rather than to be saddled with every worry?* The talk of her father's house had her worrying about Miriam again, though there had been nothing in her father's or aunt's letters to give her any alarm. And she worried for her brothers, that they would become strangers to her. And she wondered whether her father was working too hard and if he would finally consider hiring a curate.

Then she thought of Louisa-Margaretta with some worry but also with jealousy. Her friend had the money and connections to enjoy the haut ton. Judith, even if her lodgings had been in London, could never have afforded to live a fashionable life. Of course, Percival was worried about that Mr Fortescue character, but it seemed that Louisa-Margaretta had always been able to take care of herself.

*Except for that one occasion,* Judith reminded herself. Years ago, Louisa-Margaretta had stayed in London, met an unsuitable gentleman, and come so close to scandal that her parents decided to whisk her off to the country. Louisa-Margaretta always described herself as quite recovered from that first love, but Judith continued to wonder. She had seen a look of rapture come onto her friend's face when she heard anyone speak the name "Isaac" aloud, a look that was never repeated for anyone else. That showed that Louisa-Margaretta, for all her fortune and wit, was just as susceptible as a younger woman might have been to heartbreak.

Judith was not permitted to be lovesick or foolhardy. Instead of being cared for by wealthy parents who could run about the country, snatching her out of harm's way, Judith had been forced to break things off herself when she was on the brink of an unsuitable marriage. Thank goodness she and Mr Morgan Ramsbury had never officially been engaged. Then again, if she had allowed him to take things that far, perhaps she would have even more memories of him. And her memories would be far less proper.

Thinking of that loss almost made her cry, though instead, she twisted a handkerchief and walked faster. She would surely arrive back well before lunch at that rate. Louisa-Margaretta had always promised her that the bitterness of being crossed in love would fade. But that was a false promise, one Judith suspected had not even been true for her friend. Instead, her heart was sick in different seasons, at different times of day. The previous day, she had not dwelt on Mr Ramsbury, but today, without Mercy to occupy her, the memories were playing before her as if they were new.

Lunch for Mercy would be with the superintendent, and she did not wish to join. But she reached the house so quickly that she had to stop herself from going in. Instead, she sat next to the kitchen garden. If anyone asked her, she would say she felt faint, as the day was growing hot, and she did not wish to give any trouble. That would be plausible enough. She took out her tiny Bible so that nobody could accuse her of idleness. Piety, she felt, was the one weapon she had against people like the superintendent. For all his flaws, he did at least claim to be God-fearing, and if that were true, he could hardly fault her for a moment of prayer.

She heard his voice on the porch and could have smiled, for he was speaking of the Lord, though in a tone that Judith reasoned God would not particularly favor.

"I have dozens of charges," the superintendent said, "as well as a family of my own to care for. We are not going to be the subject of gossip or of chaos simply because the last week could have been worse."

Bathsheba murmured something Judith couldn't make out, but she could hear from Margaret's reaction that it had not been a declaration of filial piety.

"Bathsheba," Margaret said, her tone measured. "We must consider all the implications. If we were to send the child away, what kind of life would she have?"

"People send children away every day," the superintendent said. "That is why foundling hospitals exist, and I must acknowledge that in certain circumstances, they are the best place."

"Surely not a foundling hospital," said Margaret.

That time, Bathsheba's voice was clear. "I would rather die. We can never take her to such a place."

"That is the place for a child without parents, particularly a child without a father," said the superintendent.

A shadow was thrown over them, and Judith heard a new voice. She had no desire to make her presence felt. Apparently, the infant had caused even more turmoil than she would have believed. For days, she had simply assumed the Lambs would keep the little one. After all, they cared for dozens of people already. They had a great deal of responsibility and one daughter who was already grown. *What would an infant add to such a life, particularly if they can afford a wet nurse?* It would be easy.

"I thought I heard talk of a foundling hospital," said the doctor, and Judith winced. Of course the doctor would think he had to have his say rather than just leaving it to the Lambs.

"My father has been saying that the child has no parents," growled Bathsheba. "He wishes to kill her by leaving her at such a place."

"Thou cannot even consider it," said the doctor with venom in his voice. "It would be akin to murder."

The superintendent was nearly roaring. "I always act with consideration! As I am doing here, for the protection of all, and even for this poor nameless child!"

A gasp came from behind Judith, and she noticed that Joyce was there with the infant. It seemed strange that the little girl did not have a name. Perhaps, since the family was apparently considering foundling hospitals, they had not thought they should be the ones to christen her.

Joyce must have had the same thought as Judith, to enjoy a moment of fresh air in the kitchen garden, but she had overheard the same argument that had captured Judith's attention. The Lambs and the doctor were exchanging some rather ugly barbs.

Judith's impulse to protect the ears of someone who might not understand but was very much the subject of conversation came to the fore just as it would have with Mercy.

"Let's take the little one over to the tree," she said to the nurse. "She should not have to hear herself spoken of in those terms."

"Ugly words for religious folk," complained Joyce. "Here. Hold her for a minute, will you?"

When they were settled against the tree, there was no longer anything to hear, as after the door slammed, they saw the doctor go striding off. He stopped for a moment to stare at them then continued across the lawn.

"He's fond of this one, he is," said Joyce with a half-smile. "Sure, he's in a sour mood, but he does love a baby. Some men do. My husband didn't take to them, not before he became a father. After that, he couldn't do enough for the little ones."

"I am sure being a father is lovely," said Judith, striving for politeness. As long as she stayed under the tree with them, there was a chance the Lambs would be too distracted by their argument to call her in to lunch.

"Not always, dear," said Joyce. "And I've got to tell you I won't be using these Christian names like folks here do. No, thank you. I would call you Miss Haddington, only they seem to think the only respectful thing here is disrespectful. Strange way to live."

"Yes, it is. At least, at first," said Judith, but her companion was not listening.

"Not easy, being a father, and being a mother is harder. I learned early on, nursing children. I wouldn't have one of my own every year if I took in others. So I did, see? They've brought them to me from London, every year, for the past fifteen. It was good, as it happened, that I'd just weaned one when our little darling here arrived."

"And if she gets sent to a foundling hospital?"

Joyce laughed. "No real chance of that, is there? Certainly not. They won't be taking her anywhere. Five of my own, I have, and that's all, though I've been married these seventeen years. Told my sister she should do the same, but she never listened, and she married later. Ten, she has, and eleven soon, though it's too much to feed so many, even if I help her."

Judith wanted to be heartened by the way the woman had dismissed the talk of the foundling hospital, but she could not be so confident.

"I am also worried she would die at a foundling hospital," Judith said, stroking the baby's cheek. "It would be so much better for her to be with a family... any family. And at any rate, if the Lambs could not keep her, they have a million acquaintances who could. I hardly know any of the ladies of their church, yet I can name three who have taken in children and would take in more. I can't think why they don't consider that."

"They don't consider it because they wish to keep her here, dearie," said Joyce. "And so they will, I'll wager. But you said there are other families?"

"Many, of their own faith, who would take her. Perhaps the superintendent was too angry to think of them."

The baby chortled, and her nurse joined in. "Yes, well, I suppose he has a right to be angry. But it will all be well in time."

Hearing it from Joyce's lips, Judith could almost believe it. Almost.

# 16

Another sluggish morning for Mercy, and Judith would have taken the opportunity to sleep. She had been awakened by some sort of commotion during the night. The place was big enough that they were rarely disturbed by what happened in other wings, but she heard what she recognised as Archibald Finch's most furious voice. He was destroying something, and he spared no thought for the many sleeping inhabitants of the buildings around him. The night had been still and not cold, perfect for open windows, but Judith regretted the tirade she had been subjected to. She wondered if it had also kept Mercy awake, though at the time, she could have sworn her charge was sleeping.

Only, now she heard cries then more commotion, so instead of sleeping in, she spent precious minutes getting them both dressed so they could go down and see what had happened. Judith could not think why Joyce would have brought the tiny baby out in the cold morning air, all the way across the lawn, to a place where she would surely be less safe and much more of a disturbance.

That time, they were not the first to reach the steps. It took Judith only a minute to see that she was mistaken about Joyce. The baby was nothing like the other one. It was smaller, its cries were weaker, and the cloth it was wrapped in was something delicate surrounded by a coarser blanket on the outside.

Betsey, one of the kitchen maids, would have been up early. She was holding the baby in her arms, but she looked terrified.

"Judith," she said, though in easier moments, she would have remembered she was supposed to address both Judith and Mercy. "I just came out, and the baby was here, honest, just now. And I didn't know what to do, so I picked it up."

Peggy joined them, along with two of the women she usually helped in the morning, Deborah and Charity, both of whom tended to rise early. It was rare, especially outside a meal, to see everyone absorbed by the same sight. But all of the women had eyes for nothing but the child.

"Come in," said Judith, pushing the doors open wide. "It's cold here. We may as well go in to breakfast."

Betsey did not move, still looking shocked that she was holding an unknown child in her arms, and Judith snapped, "Somebody bring the baby."

Mercy took the child to her, and she had warmth in her eyes. Judith did not want to tear the baby away, especially since the rocking seemed to do something to still the little one's cries. But she also knew that milk was what the baby needed most of all.

"Peggy," she said, trying to keep her voice low. "If Betsey stays with Charity and Deborah, can you run across and fetch Joyce Garvey? She can feed two children instead of one, at least this morning."

Peggy's face was pale. "Yes," she said. "I will run."

And she did, much faster than Judith would have expected. Peggy truly had grown stronger during her time at the home, and she hoped the older wet nurse would be able to keep up before the baby grew desperate with hunger.

*This is a very new baby,* Judith realised. It seemed much younger than the other one, its face still gaunt and pink. Or perhaps it was because of underfeeding.

"Come to the parlor," she said. "We can't allow any more of the chill air, poor thing."

There was still very little light, and Judith lit the fire herself. They would never have bothered in summer, and after some deliberation, Judith decided to send Deborah to get the wood. Although at times, Deborah's melancholy slowed her movements, she had nearly the grace and quickness Peggy had shown, and before anyone else arrived, Judith had got a tolerably good fire built up. She stepped back carefully, locking the grate that had been constructed just for that room. Nobody who wished to get near the fire could do so without a key, but other than that, it looked ordinary, and though it smoked a bit, it certainly warmed up the room.

Bathsheba, Judith was surprised to see, was in her dressing gown, hugging the older baby to her. She must have walked like that all the way to spare Joyce some trouble.

"Make haste," said Judith.

"No haste, just milk," she said, and she slowly held out her arms to Mercy, who surrendered the child as if in a dream. The baby's jaws seemed strong, and a sigh went through the room. Judith realised she had wondered whether the child was abandoned because it was dying, but the child was plainly hungry. This baby would live and be strong like the other one.

Though it only took one look at Margaret's face for her to realise the child's life was not the only matter of some worry.

"Where did this child come from?" asked Margaret, looking nearly as confused as Mercy did.

"Why do they keep bringing them here?" Peggy added, looking less sad but equally mystified. "It's as if everyone has learned that this is a place of sanctuary."

Nobody answered, all of them gazing at the little child. The baby had its cheek pressed up to Joyce, still drinking a great deal as the nurse stroked its fine hair.

*Sanctuary, indeed.*

**17**

———

It was some time before anyone thought to call for the doctor. The infant seemed so much revived from his milk—they had confirmed it was a boy, a little Moses of sorts, safe among women. At one point, Joyce even amused them all by feeding both babes at once, showing how it could be done without allowing them to knock heads.

"I've done it before, and I can do it again," she said. "God is merciful. I was just where I needed to be for this strong little chap."

"He might be sick," said Bathsheba. "Should I not go find the doctor?"

That made Joyce laugh. "Look at the chap. As healthy as can be now he's had his milk. He'll be able to wail just as well as the other soon enough. You'll see."

"I should go for the doctor," insisted Bathsheba.

But Margaret shook her head. "Absolutely not. We can send someone else."

"I'll go," said Judith. There were more than enough people about to keep careful eyes on Mercy. And though she thought Mercy's eyes were still a bit mournful, falling as they were on Judith and Bathsheba as she perhaps tried to make out their words, she had been more in spirits than usual since her brief spell of holding the baby.

"I'll go with you," offered Bathsheba with a smile.

"Very well," said Margaret. "But I do not like that someone came onto our grounds with a baby and nobody took any notice at all. The two of you are to stay together at all times, not to stray from each other's sides for an instant. Do you understand?"

Bathsheba shrugged, but Judith answered with a nod.

"Yes," she said. "I understand."

When they set out, Judith looked about the grounds, but she could see nobody lurking, and the fog of the morning had already lifted. She was surprised to see Bathsheba wandering off in the wrong direction.

"We should go find the doctor directly," she said gently. "To the house?"

"He has not been living there for some time." Bathsheba laughed. "I can tell that the pleasures of our table mean little to thee, Judith."

Judith blushed. "It is nothing against your parents' hospitality. Thy parents' hospitality. The kindness of your whole family. I mean to say—"

"My mother decided it would be best for him not to live under the same roof with, well, quite so many people," said Bathsheba archly, and Judith almost smiled. For all the sympathy Margaret claimed to feel toward the young doctor, at heart, perhaps she did agree with Judith. But if she was so sure the doctor's prickly nature warranted a separate living arrangement, Judith wondered why she did not pressure her husband to simply get rid of him. Before the previous day's row, she would have said it was because the doctor and the superintendent often agreed on how to run things, how to treat people, and in general, how to live. But the previous day, the doctor had seemed to disagree with everyone, perhaps the superintendent most of all, and he certainly was not polite or respectful in the way he aired his opinions.

"I wonder that I never knew he lived here. You said he has been living here some time?"

"Since before I went away."

"Oftentimes, I feel like nothing happens here without everyone else knowing of it at once," Judith mused, trying to walk as quickly as Bathsheba without losing her in the woods.

"Are we all such gossips? I can assure thee this must not be quite true."

"No, not gossips," Judith hastened to reassure her. "Only we are all so much together. Conversations tend toward the little things. Meals we shared or what is growing well in the garden or even the fine carriage of one of our visitors. It is not like other places, where government or society is more part of the general conversation."

"Do you miss those conversations?" asked Bathsheba. For the first time, she seemed interested in what Judith was saying.

"Not exactly." Judith noticed the young woman seemed relieved to hear it. "I lived in the country for most of my life, at any rate, so what was happening in London always felt rather distant. But I do miss literature and music. Perhaps it is too secular for many here, but I must confess that my time with Mercy has allowed me to remember my acquaintance with Mr Bach with great pleasure."

"You knew him?"

"No, of course not! Though I felt as if I did. When my sister teased me, she said that I was going to go see whether my good friend Mr Bach was receiving callers, and it did feel that way sometimes."

Bathsheba nodded, but she seemed distracted. "He has not risen," she said, "or left his cabin. Perhaps he is ill."

They had come to a small cottage, and Bathsheba was standing with her hand on the gate, peering at the windows.

"Perhaps he did leave."

Bathsheba replied, "The gate is open, and if he had left, the gate would be closed."

She seemed quite sure on that point.

"Perhaps he will not wish to be disturbed. But if he is ill, somebody really ought to see to him. We will have to call one of those women from the village or send to London for a different doctor if he is truly unwell."

Bathsheba gave a little smile, though Judith noticed that worry had crept into her brow. "He would not much like that, to be sure."

Judith was more annoyed. The doctor thought himself quite superior to anyone else who claimed knowledge of healing. At one time, in a moment of humility, he had admitted his prior knowledge and expertise on "remedies for madness" had all turned out to be far less useful than a good hot bath.

"I will go in and see," said Bathsheba firmly. "I will send for thee if we need to find someone of that sort."

"It is not seemly. We must both go."

She saw one of the gardeners walking across the lawn and called to him. He looked at her with surprise. Generally, it was understood that those working inside the buildings and outside seldom spoke, even if they were all in some sort of service. Though Judith had seen many divides fall away during her time in the strange place, that was not one of them, and she wondered whether he even knew her name.

He was one of the more experienced gardeners, and it was largely down to him that they had such a bountiful kitchen garden.

"We need someone to help us see to the doctor," she said. "We need his help, but he would normally be awake, and it seems he is not. Could you go and see whether he is ill?"

"Of course," he said with a smile for both of them.

He was not long, and he closed the door carefully before speaking with them again.

"We need to go find the superintendent," he said, clearing his throat. "I saw him earlier. I believe he might have been off after our William."

"I hadn't heard William was wandering this morning," said Judith, frowning. She wondered whether the events of the previous evening had been disturbing to the young man. She had been so taken up with Mercy then with both the infants in the morning that she had not given much thought as to how the men were taking things.

"Well, I'm not sure he was," said the gardener. "Only I saw—"

"What is wrong with Ludlow?" asked Bathsheba.

Judith realised she was one of the few people around them who used the doctor's name. To most, he was just "the doctor," as they seemed uncomfortable addressing him with only a name and no title when his profession was such a large reason for his being there with them.

"He has passed on," said the man, looking away from both of them. His meaning was perfectly clear.

Judith tried to hold Bathsheba back, but she flew past Judith to the door, where she threw herself against it, grasping for the handle.

The gardener caught her, and Judith saw with some satisfaction that he did not mean to let her go.

"It is no sight for a young lady," he said. "It is distressing, and I will not allow thee to pass, Bathsheba."

She fought and twisted until Judith saw Margaret coming down the path.

"It is not true!" she nearly screamed. "It cannot be true, Ludlow, dead!"

Margaret gave a sharp intake of breath. She touched her daughter's face but asked the gardener, "He is dead?"

"Yes."

"Judith," said Margaret sharply, and Judith felt something pressed into her palm.

Bathsheba began to scream and struggle again. It was a key, just one, not the large set Margaret carried with her at all times.

When she finally caught her meaning, she rushed over to the door, locked it, and stepped away before she nodded at Margaret.

Bathsheba ran to the door again, but she could not open it, so she sank down against it, wailing.

Margaret went over to her. "Come, Bathsheba. Come."

Judith realised she was trembling. "I will go for the superintendent."

"Thank you," the gardener said shakily.

**18**

———

Judith did not know where to find the superintendent, and after she walked away from Bathsheba's cries, she hesitated between the man's home and the large building where he spent much of his waking time.

After the events of the previous evening, he really should be looking in on all the men. But if he had been up early in the morning, chasing William, he might be tired, and if he had gone so far as to find a horse, he might be gone still. Finding a horse and perhaps borrowing a dog from one of their nearest neighbors was the only way to cope with William sometimes. Judith hated to think of it as hunting, but really, it was, since William had the agility of a fox but was considerably less predictable in his wanderings. Most everyone who tried to go on foot ended up falling back and losing him. Judith was hardly an excellent rider, but sometimes, even she had been dispatched to seek him out when nobody else who could manage riding through the woods and crossing streams was at hand. Conversation was usually enough to lure him in the opposite direction, and food was more than enough to ensure he returned eventually.

Judith eventually decided on the building where the superintendents lived, where she had believed that the doctor was still in residence. It had so many rooms, especially in the back, that she ought to be forgiven for not noticing that particular change. She did know which room served as a sort of private library for both superintendents, and that was where she found the man who had the highest role at the home. He was sitting, quill in hand, looking at what appeared to be a book of accounts. Judith wished she could have spoken to him of such a prosaic matter, one that had nothing to do with death, and she could not keep herself from trying.

"I am happy to help with the accounts if I may assist you," she said.

The superintendent frowned, looking up at her. "Judith, why would you offer such a thing? We have dozens of individuals here, a large staff, and hundreds of subscribers. It would be beyond you."

*It would not,* thought Judith, but she only frowned. "I often helped my father," she said. "In both parishes, his responsibilities were great, and I am sure that I could learn—"

The superintendent closed the book. "This is nonsense. Is there anything else?"

Judith found herself trembling. She could not avoid the purpose of the errand, then. "The doctor," she said. "One of the gardeners went to look in on him, and he is dead."

The superintendent sighed. "Did you see him yourself, or did you only speak to the gardener? Why would he go to a young woman with this news, not to me?"

Judith frowned. "Bathsheba and I went to see the doctor.

There has been another foundling, and we wanted his expertise."

The superintendent gave a chuckle. "Another foundling! Surely not."

"Yes," said Judith slowly, unsure how to interpret the man's response. "The baby seems healthy. But Bathsheba and I wished to be sure."

The superintendent did not respond for some moments, and Judith's eyes flickered toward the door. Since her errand had been dispatched, she had better get back to Mercy. It was impossible to be sure how she would take the news, and Judith ought to be there in case Mercy needed the soothing power of Bach or friendship.

"Had he any other family, do you know?"

"Yes. He has a brother. They were not on good terms, but that hardly matters now. We shall have to send someone to London to inform him."

**19**

L ouisa-Margaretta hated morning callers, and she tried to be at home to them as little as possible.

Since Federica wished to rest more, many of the tactful ladies stayed away. Consequently, the people who did come to bother her were the most insensitive bores. Louisa-Margaretta, who was never ill, was constantly claiming sick headaches with a perfectly straight face in order that her friend not be obliged to lie for her.

"I see you would rather not help me face them today, Louie," said Federica after breakfast, yawning as she and her friend looked out the window. Louisa-Margaretta had just declared that she would be heading up the stairs at the first sight of a fine headdress.

"I shall help you recover from them," she declared, her voice full of noble intent while she grinned wickedly. "Then next time, I shall behave abominably, and perhaps that way, we can get them to stop calling."

"Did you have ever so many callers in the countryside?"

"No, I had one friend, and we were rather quiet."

Federica smiled. "That sounds a great deal like my life in the country. It is why I love it."

"Yes."

Louisa-Margaretta had still not forgotten the cold of winter that she had declared intolerable. And in Derbyshire, it was snowy as well as cold, and at times, it seemed as if she would never again get to go anywhere amusing. But for all that, the company made up for most things. It might have been quite dreary without Judith.

She wondered about Judith. Perhaps if everything had been different, Louisa-Margaretta would have been able to take Cousin Morgan up on his advice to write and sell music. She was forever thinking of clever little rhymes that could be part of a song, and Judith wrote music just as easily. She had no idea how to go about selling such a thing, but her father could help. And if the two of them were able to sell enough, they might even endeavor to live on their own. Louisa-Margaretta was in the haut ton, being eyed hungrily by a bunch of bores, and Judith was in a madhouse. Things could hardly be worse.

Though, of course, they could be more scandalous.

"I can't think why he is calling when you are never at home to him," said Federica. "He never carries on this way with any of the other young ladies."

"Who?"

"Oh, your Mr Fortescue. Only look at him there on the stair. He looks very ill indeed. Perhaps he is not sleeping for thinking of you."

Louisa-Margaretta shoved her friend just as hard as she had when they were children, and Federica laughed.

"I can't name this baby for you if you will insist on pushing me, Louie."

"Louie, as a name for your baby?"

"Why not? Louis or Louisa. I'm afraid Louisa-Margaretta is too much of a mouthful. If none of my children can say it now, they will not learn it by the time the baby is old enough to be offended."

A knock sounded on their door, but instead of the housekeeper, it was Federica's maid. In the hushed conference, Louisa-Margaretta's friend's voice grew serious.

"I see," she said. She came over to Louisa-Margaretta and touched her arm. "You need to stay here. We must be at home for Mr Fortescue today."

Louisa-Margaretta's first thought was that there would be a proposal... another one. Perhaps it would be in deadly earnest, before witnesses, too, though she hardly liked the thought of her friend hearing the man's improper thoughts. Before she could beg Federica to stay, the man himself was shown in, and Federica greeted him.

"I am so sorry for your loss," she said. "I have only just heard."

He barely nodded, coming over to sit next to Louisa-Margaretta instead. "Thank you," he managed, and she sat up straight.

Though she hated it, her thoughts had flown immediately to her brother. "Percival? Is he not well? Is that what you have come to tell me?"

She remembered how angry she had been with her brother the last time she spoke with him and how rash his words must have sounded. If he knew Louisa-Margaretta's feelings, he might have thought to save her from Mr Fortescue. She had sudden vision of him challenging the man, of Mr Fortescue getting the better of Percival in a duel.

"No," he choked out. "It is not Percival. It is my own brother."

"Your brother? Who?"

"He is a doctor in an institution. Well, *was* a doctor. They have just told me. He is dead."

Then Mr Fortescue was weeping as if he were a child, and Federica left the room without a look at her friend. Louisa-Margaretta found her hands clutched between his, and she frowned as she tried to remember anything she had heard about a brother.

"I am very sorry," she murmured. She felt she had, perhaps, heard something. The brother, of course, would be a second son, so he would have had no fortune of his own. Still, that was not enough to make a man bury himself in the countryside. No, there was something else. It was from her mother. That was it.

Louisa-Margaretta's mother was not a gossip, but she was not happy that both Peggy and Judith were going to be living in proximity to a man Louisa-Margaretta realised could only be the wayward younger brother of Mr Fortescue. The younger brother, Mr Ludlow Fortescue, was notorious for having seduced a young woman then refusing to marry her even when she was quite ruined. The young woman had fallen ill and lost the child, and by that time, he had married her, but the damage to his reputation was done. And the poor woman sank into madness, ending up in the very same madhouse where Peggy and Judith were living.

That made her sit straighter, and though the gentleman did not release her hands, he did gather himself enough to look into her face.

"Is everyone safe?" she asked. "Was it only your brother, or did others die with him?"

"What do you mean?" he asked dully. "Others?"

Louisa-Margaretta was angry enough for her own tears to start, but she fought them back. "I imagine some madman in that place ran amok with a knife and your brother was a victim. But were there others amongst the dead?"

"I do not know how he died. The message only said that he had not woken from a sound sleep after a night of difficulties and that some other doctor had seen him to confirm that he would not have suffered."

A knot that had wrapped around her chest eased for a moment. Her heart was still fluttering. *In an instant, to lose Peggy and Judith both!* And she realised they were precious to her—Peggy because she had always been kind and because Louisa-Margaretta had abandoned her in an hour of great distress and confusion. With Judith, it was a simpler sadness. If Judith were lost to the world, Louisa-Margaretta would have lost a part of herself. She could not conceive of that. It would be as if a stranger had walked in and told her that both her legs were to be amputated.

"The others are safe," she said. "The others who live in that strange place?"

"Yes, much good may it do them," said the man, wrenching his hands free and standing suddenly. He began to pace. "That place never deserved my brother, and their Quaker ways are certainly most unnatural. If they somehow drove him to his death, I would not be surprised."

"Did they ever manage to cure his wife?" asked Louisa-Margaretta. As she saw it, the lady was the one who had truly lost out. Since the Fortescue brothers had parents from distant lands, however high in society they moved, there was still something of the exotic about them. And of course, the ladies of the ton had not held back in their criticisms of both the Continent and the Orient after the poor lady was ruined. It seemed that a fair English gentleman was the only husband one might deem safe and respectable, which of course, only made the young ladies love Mr Fortescue all the more.

"No," said Mr Fortescue, rubbing his forehead. "You knew of her, then? She has never been cured, another reason they ought never to have gone. All those years, and for nothing."

"Perhaps it was a sort of penance," said Louisa-Margaretta dreamily, smoothing her skirts and trying to keep her voice even so as not to upset the frantic man in front of her. She never quite felt she had done anything so wrong as to require atonement, but she was sure she could not pity a seducer forced to answer for his actions. After all, it was a rare-enough occurrence.

"My brother never needed any sort of penance," the man nearly spat. "That was the trouble with him. Good to his soul, to his bones, and now he is lost. And we had not spoken for years, not a word! Oh, to lose him forever."

Louisa-Margaretta looked at her hands, which she had folded carefully, embarrassed for Mr Fortescue. *Is this true grief, then?* She had never had the misfortune to lose anyone terribly close to her. It seemed cruel to say, but when a relative of hers died, she had never felt the same sting she would have felt for her parents, her brothers, or even a beloved horse. If poor Mr Fortescue were so bereft as to believe his wayward brother was some kind of martyr, she was not going to argue with him. But she could hardly pretend that she agreed.

"I am very sorry," she murmured. "Would you like some tea?"

Then he laughed, which was worse. He went between crying and laughing, until he was on the sofa with her again, that time caressing her face with his hands.

She knew she ought to ask him to stop. To be considered

perfectly proper, she should run away and remove the temptation. But his hands were both strong and gentle, his face so near hers, so unutterably handsome, that she could not think of pulling away.

"Oh, you," he said. "I will avenge my brother's death, then you will have to marry me, my love. There is nobody like you on earth, and do not think I am not going to profit by this lesson. We shall be married as soon as it can be decently arranged."

She did not agree to it exactly, but she did let him kiss her, or perhaps she kissed him. It was so long since she had kissed anyone that it ought to have been awkward, only it was not. His kisses were hot and full of passion, and before she knew it, she was embracing him.

It could have been intentional that one of the servants made a bit of a clatter in the hall, or perhaps it was some scheme of Federica's. Louisa-Margaretta tried to leap away, and after a moment, Mr Fortescue let her go. Then she did ring for tea because she needed an excuse to stay away from him. He posed a danger to her reputation.

When Federica came in, following the servant who brought the tea, Louisa-Margaretta contrived to keep her there. She could not ever allow herself to be alone with Mr Fortescue.

But if she stayed in London, it was sure to happen again. Moments could be stolen anywhere—in parks, in public galleries, or in dimly lit corridors just beyond the eyes of the host.

"Federica," she said when Mr Fortescue finally took his leave. "I must find Percival. The two of us are going to the country."

**20**

Louisa-Margaretta went to tea expecting to have some sort of serious conversation. But when she saw Peggy and Judith, the two people whose deaths she had imagined only days earlier, she ended up holding fast to the edges of her chair, unable to speak.

"There now, Louisa-Margaretta," said Peggy archly. "It isn't such a bad place, you know. Or does the very thought of madness give you the vapours? I was quite sure you were tougher than that."

"She is. It is something else," said Judith, missing nothing about her friend.

"When they said the doctor had died," managed Louisa-Margaretta, "I was worried for you both. That is why I arranged a special visit."

Judith frowned. "A special visit to see we are both alive?"

"There was little news about the death. Mr Fortescue came to call on me, and he told me that his brother was the only person to perish. But I was still uneasy. If either of you were in danger here, I am not very sure that in London, I would know."

For a moment, there was no sound but the pouring of the tea as Peggy served the younger ladies and herself.

"We are not in danger," she said. "But, Louisa-Margaretta, allowing visits from the elder Mr Fortescue is very dangerous. His reputation is plenty well known, and it is not a flattering one."

"You sound just like Percival." Louisa-Margaretta finally allowed herself to feel angry. It was much easier than admitting she had been feeling sad, that a fear for her friend and sister-in-law had made her lose sleep until she could see them.

"I am sure Percival knows even more of his reputation," said Judith, her tone reminding Louisa-Margaretta that she and Percival had not gotten on well recently—or ever, perhaps.

Percival had always loved fun, but he had none of his sister's toughness, so that gave him little in common with a young woman who had spent her childhood tidying prayer books and looking to Bach for entertainment.

"His reputation is beside the point," said Louisa-Margaretta impatiently. "He will end up going mad and being put here himself if he does not learn more about how his brother died. He says he suspects Mr Ludlow Fortescue was murdered."

Peggy shook her head. "That cannot be. The doctor was respected here, and what's more, he was needed."

"Yes, by a lot of people with rather violent proclivities!"

"They are most violent to themselves," said Judith. "It is rare for any violent act to be attempted against one of us here, and the consequences are always swift. Besides, the doctor's cabin was locked the night he died."

"Nobody could possibly get in through a locked door,"

said Louisa-Margaretta. "Certainly, it is impossible that he let the killer in or that they used a window!"

"And then he locked it again after he died?" asked Peggy. "Really, my dear. I know you have seen murders before, but what happened here was a tragedy, no more and no less."

"And I am sure there have been no other suspicious happenings lately," said Louisa-Margaretta, desperate to convince at least one of the women of Mr Fortescue's suspicions, though she was not sure she believed them herself. Something about the circumstances gave her pause. Even though she was far from believing the strange claim that the doctor was a selfless man with a good heart, it did seem plausible to her that in treating madness, he might have made some grave error of judgement. After all, he was fairly young and had apparently always been healthy. Perhaps he had ignored a particular danger posed by a villain until it was far too late.

Peggy and Judith exchanged glances so slight they might have passed unnoticed in a different parlor. But Louisa-Margaretta noticed at once.

"There *has* been something happening here," she declared. "Something that is suspicious and unexplained and certainly connected intimately to the murder of this man!"

"It is not necessarily suspicious," said Judith gently. "And there are some explanations. But the babies are tiny, and I do truly think there can be no connection."

"And the babies are to live here?" asked Peggy, putting down her tea. "Oh, Judith, have you heard?"

"No," said Judith carefully. "I have been wanting to ask, of course, but there was such a row last time. I believe nobody likes to think of it when we are all concerned about mourning the doctor properly."

"Was he a wonderful doctor?" asked Louisa-Margaretta. She wanted to know why babies had entered into the conversation, but she was also quite curious as to what the actual Mr Fortescue seemed to people who were not his near relations.

"Many of our guests are much improved," replied Judith.

"Yes," Peggy said without hesitation. "Of course he was a wonderful doctor! When I was first here, I was sick so very often. And he always listened carefully, always found something for me, even if it was only a hot drink. He promised that when my spirit was well my lungs would be also, and he was right."

Louisa-Margaretta peered at Peggy. Her admiration, to be sure, was sincere, but she needed another opinion. "Judith?"

"We should not speak ill of the dead."

"But if you *were* to speak ill of the dead. Just for a moment. Was he the sort of man a person would want to murder?"

"No," said Judith rather too quickly, flushing. "But he could be difficult, at least at times. Particularly with our, well, our blessings."

"Blessings?"

"Margaret Lamb doesn't like us calling them foundlings," said Peggy. "There have been two so far."

"So far?" asked Louisa-Margaretta and Judith in unison.

"I feel quite sure that they will not be the only ones. Babies left on the steps for our care. And they have been well-loved here."

"In part thanks to you," said Judith. "Peggy is paying a wet nurse to live here so they do not go hungry. It has been marvelous for both of them, but we would be in difficulties without her generosity."

Louisa-Margaretta frowned. Her family's money was supporting the wet nurse, then—although not directly. "How marvelous," she said, looking from Peggy to Judith. "Well, it sounds as if the foundlings are a rather strange occurrence. Do let me know how I might assist."

Judith looked down. "We are all quite well here," she murmured. "Thou—you—really do not need to trouble yourself about us, Louisa-Margaretta."

"Nonsense. I need information, and you need funds for ever more nurses, apparently, if there are to be more ugly little baskets dropped at your doors."

"Children," Peggy said, scolding her.

"Quite."

"Please," said Judith, looking between the two of them.

Louisa-Margaretta, assured her former friend was quite alive, was amused to see Judith becoming alarmed over Peggy's rude responses and Louisa-Margaretta's aggressive offers.

"Peggy and I must return to our duties. One of the young ladies who is normally a great help to us has felt too ill since the doctor's death to be in company, and another attendant left only a month ago."

"I cannot go away with so little," said Louisa-Margaretta, alarmed. "Surely you could spare me another moment."

Peggy gave her a curt smile. "We are in great need of assistance," she said. "But not only money is needed. Instead, we need a young woman who will live here and tend to our residents with the greatest possible care. Would that not be an excellent way for you to acquire the information you so desire?"

Louisa-Margaretta laughed. "I, work in a Quaker madhouse? I cannot begin to imagine such a lowering occupation."

Judith, for the first time, appeared offended. "That would not be my description," she said. "And Peggy is quite right. We are very short just now. Will you help us?"

Louisa-Margaretta remembered when they had all left Wycliff Castle. Peggy was in quite a state, and Judith, who had been practically a stranger, had declared she would not leave her side. She stayed with Peggy, enduring who knew what torture in the place they called a "home"—*What a name!*—and Louisa-Margaretta had gone to London to enjoy balls and high society.

She practically slammed her teacup down. "Fine," she said. "But the moment someone asks me to empty a chamber pot, I shall leave."

**21**

———————

Louisa-Margaretta got little by way of conversation out of Peggy. And that would have been acceptable, had she been able to find conversation anywhere else.

On the first morning of her official employment with the home, she saw that all the ladies got out their workbaskets after breakfast. Louisa-Margaretta thought she would be able to manage a drawing room. After all, as negligent as she had always been with her own work, she had learned a thing or two from Mama. She was even an expert at making polite little comments as she pretended to pick at threads. As it happened, she could go on that way for quite a long time, rarely making any progress. She always told her mother that she was saving them money on materials, an idea that amused Papa to no end. Mama was always working on little things that were both beautiful and functional. She needed an acceptable way to express her natural generosity, and though her gifts were made of fine material, even the poorest parishioner would be forced to accept them out of politeness.

Louisa-Margaretta thought she was doing rather well, in fact. She made little comments, though nobody said anything back—except for Timofea, who would go on with her irrelevant little utterances. At least, Louisa-Margaretta thought, being ignored in a drawing room was a role she would be comfortable playing.

But Esther, a woman with an unlined face and hair that was completely grey, giving her a rather ethereal look, was the first to complain.

"It is cold here," she said. "We need a fire."

Marla, a younger woman sitting by the fire, let out a most unladylike noise of disapproval. "Full summer, and she says she needs a fire. Some of us weren't raised in palaces, you know."

"Palaces are very drafty," burst out Timofea, the youngest of the bunch. "In fact, anyone who had been raised in a palace would certainly learn to tolerate a great deal of cold and heat. They are too large to be built to modern standards, and many of them are very old."

Marla glared at her. "So now we're supposed to feel sorry for the poor little princes and princesses, are we? Well, if that's the case, I'll take some of your finest thread."

Clarinda, who rarely spoke, pushed Marla's hand away from Timofea's workbasket.

"Don't touch me!" shrieked Marla, throwing herself at the silent Clarinda.

Louisa-Margaretta tried to separate them, but it was useless. The two of them had ended up on the floor, the contents of their workbaskets spilling everywhere, as Timofea sat back and cowered.

The spell was only broken by Esther trying to break her way into the grate. It was covered with a special iron fitting, the likes of which Louisa-Margaretta had never seen before.

The idea was that the fires should be functional, but any madwoman who wished to stick her hand into the fire must be prevented from doing so. And it did work to keep Esther out. She was not able to work the lock, but she did succeed in using a rather long needle to knock down one of the logs that was supposed to be kept out of reach, which toppled the poker, and that made enough of a noise that the whole room stopped to look at her.

"Enough!" Louisa-Margaretta took advantage of the temporary silence. "I have a great deal of fine thread in my own workbasket, though I did not come from a palace. Any person who sits quietly with her work will receive some of it. The longer the silence, the more thread I am prepared to contribute."

"Like a nunnery in here," said Marla, who refused the offer of thread. She was, however, much quieter, though she seemed to be gathering the things that had once been in her workbasket rather excessively slowly.

Clarinda had not moved to gather her things at all, but Louisa-Margaretta did not go over to her seat. She hoped that by avoiding the woman, she might at least keep from provoking another outburst. Timofea rocked back and forth and also refused, though more quietly. Clarinda snatched at some of it, though she had not done any sewing, and Esther even broke off her attempts to get through the grate to have a good look at the thread.

"Louisa-Margaretta?" asked Timofea.

She was still not used to hearing her first name spoken by anyone but very close friends and family, and she disliked it.

"What is it?" she asked rather too quickly.

"Do you think you might help me with this knot?" The girl frowned.

Peggy came in just then, glaring at Louisa-Margaretta. "I would be happy to help you," she said.

As soon as she had helped her young charge, she pulled Louisa-Margaretta aside for a whispered tête-à-tête. She had hardly spoken to her the day before or that morning, but now she seemed unable to stop speaking.

"They are all terrified, and you have made a mess," she said. "I was not gone half an hour. What on earth have you been doing to them?"

"What have *you* done to them? They have no discipline, and most of the work I see here is even worse than mine."

"They are not here for needlepoint. They are here to get well. And I hardly think that will happen if each of them is made miserable by workhouse conditions."

"This is not a workhouse," hissed Louisa-Margaretta.

Peggy smiled, and Louisa-Margaretta realised that was exactly what she had been meant to say. Because Peggy's wit and weapons had always been trained on someone else, Louisa-Margaretta had rather forgotten how much hurt the woman could inflict when she felt that she had been wronged.

"Of course it is not," she said. "If it were, you would never have accepted such poor quality."

Clapping, she joined the group again. "Ladies, I am ever so sorry to have lingered in the kitchens, but I think I have finally talked my way into a lovely marrow pasty, so I do believe that it will have been worth it in the end."

A general cheer went up, and the mood lifted immediately.

The mood of the room, that was. Louisa-Margaretta's mood was as black as could be.

**22**

────────

Judith could not wait to leave the Lamb family. She had expected to rush back over and find Mercy, taking some solace in caregiving.

Instead, poor Lucy was standing at the door to the drawing room, rocking on her heels. Mercy would be in there alone. It was the time of morning when the other ladies were to be helping in the kitchen, the garden, or one of the other places where they contributed to the home. That was supposed to be in the name of helping them get well, though it was often useful in stretching the funds contributed by the home's subscribers.

"You can go into the drawing room, Lucy," said Judith. "Mercy has only ever hurt herself and the furniture. She'll not harm you."

"But I can't," said Lucy. "I can't. Oh, it's terrible, it is."

Judith walked into the room, bracing herself for the things that had once frightened her—people losing control before they could get to a chamber pot or perhaps vomiting or someone who had destroyed a painting or cut up a perfectly good gown with scissors. In other words, madness.

Those things had become less alarming to her, though she could not pretend to like them. Nothing about them was new.

But what she found was worse. Mercy sat in a chair at the window, her face devoid of any expression. It was sadder than it was on the days when she did not wish to leave her bed. Even on those days, there would still be something, like a sound or a crinkling of the brow. But Mercy had disappeared entirely into herself, and even when Judith tried to rouse her, she would do nothing, only sit with her face to the window.

The only way Judith eventually got her to move was by singing her favorite Bach cantata. The music was enough to get the woman pacing about, holding Judith's elbow, though little more happened after that.

When Judith saw that Louisa-Margaretta had come into the drawing room with some of the other ladies, she wanted to turn around. Judith was not at all used to seeing her friend in what had become her place of solace and still did not quite know how to address her. The two of them had quarreled, which might have been nothing, only after their quarrel, a year had passed. More than a year, and they had not written to each other or spoken once. Judith no longer felt sure she knew the young woman who had been living in London all that time, encouraging the attentions of men such as Mr Fortescue. Her old conviction, that Louisa-Margaretta thought Judith too poor and rather dull, came back up to the surface whenever they spoke, and she found herself wishing she were anywhere else.

"Is it always like this?" breathed Louisa-Margaretta in what must have passed as a whisper for her. "I thought I was a difficult girl, but these ladies would make my mother appreciate my occasional amiability."

"I am sure you were rarely amiable," said Judith then worried about the reaction.

But Louisa-Margaretta only laughed. "I was—whenever there was a hunt and I wanted to be allowed to go."

"So not at all outside the hunting season."

"Of course not."

Judith relaxed for a moment. Perhaps Louisa-Margaretta was not quite the grand lady of pleasure she had imagined.

"Do you still wish to hunt?" she asked. "I believe there should be somewhere you could find near here if Percival would take you. Mr Haddington, I mean! Mr Percival Haddington."

She bit her tongue. She had lived in her current home for quite a long while. Instead of forcing herself to use the Christian names they insisted on, she needed to remind herself to address gentlemen respectably.

"I would never go with him. He is terrible at hunting. But I do need to know who killed that doctor of yours. Mr Fortescue is quite beside himself."

"And what is his opinion to you?" asked Judith, trying to be gentle.

Louisa-Margaretta frowned. "Nothing. But he is grieving and much too angry to find out anything useful for himself. So I have decided to help catch the murderer."

"And this has nothing to do with your wishing to leave London? Or with fancying a man who has more or less publicly declared that he never wishes to marry anyone?"

"Please, Judith. Me, fancy a gentleman! As much as I do hope to arrange an eligible match for myself, I should never be so stupid as to fancy anyone ever again. I am not a girl, you know."

Judith nodded perhaps a little too quickly. If she allowed the conversation to go in that direction any longer, they might well end up in a discussion of her own fancies. And she did not wish her friend to bring up Mr Morgan Ramsbury because she knew Louisa-Margaretta would see at once that Judith had not recovered in that regard. If anything, her more recent loneliness and sorrow at her circumstances only made a grand romance seem especially enticing.

"Louisa-Margaretta," said Judith, her voice louder than she had intended. Seeing Timofea look over, she lowered it. "Do you know that men who fight for money often hit other things? Sacks of grain, for example, to strengthen their blows. It makes their fists tough, I suppose."

Louisa-Margaretta gave a wicked grin. "Yes, would that I could observe such a thing now, instead of being in a drawing room as torturous as any I have ever known."

Judith blushed, but it was half from anger. "Yes, well, to the doctor, I was little more than such a sack of grain. I was a convenient place for his anger, his pride, his declarations of superiority. It is exactly the kind of behavior we would not hear of if any of the ladies here were to attempt such a thing. And he was to cure us all? No, he was a wicked man, certainly not a suitable example."

She tried to get up and turn away, still disturbed by the dullness of Mercy's rocking. It was as if she knew absolutely everything about the murder, even though Judith had tried very hard to shield her. They could not keep the other ladies from talking entirely, of course, but she had hoped Mercy would not understand.

"But was he always such a horrible gorgon, Judith?" Louisa-Margaretta asked. "Or was there a moment, perhaps recently, when he was worse?"

Judith looked down at her fingers. She had been twisting a spare bit of thread in them.

"He was not so unpleasant when I first came, I think. Then again, I was so often with Peggy that I paid him very little mind."

Louisa-Margaretta looked away. "Yes. I can see that. I should have been here with Peggy. I shall make it up to her somehow."

She had not noticed that Peggy had approached her from behind, and she gasped when her sister-in-law revealed herself.

"Peggy," said Judith.

"I am very glad that thou wouldst make it up to me, Louisa-Margaretta," said Peggy, her voice clipped and clear. "I shall relieve thee here, and thou mayst go and fetch our William."

## 23

Louisa-Margaretta spent the afternoon sweating, knowing she had been sent off on a fool's errand.

Apparently, nobody but her could be spared to chase William.

"You are very healthy, and I think you can manage it," Margaret had said, the worry on her face contradicting each of her statements. "You are so young and so quick."

"And so inept when it comes to the women. Peggy is trying to teach me, but I am an abominable pupil."

If Louisa-Margaretta had said it hoping to be corrected, she would be disappointed. Margaret only nodded. "Well, it is difficult. Time is a good teacher. You would not expect to learn how to ride a horse or read Greek or do something like that in one day."

"Rome wasn't built in a day, you mean?"

"We try not to hold up Rome as an ideal," said Margaret with the barest glimmer of a smile. "Although, I suppose I did mention learning to read Greek, which is not so different in some ways."

"I am told I learned to canter in no more than an afternoon, and a thousand hours was not enough to teach me the barest bit of Greek. But I will go after him if you wish it."

Mr Crew, the farmer, was not too keen to give up his mare. "They ought to buy her. They do deal fairly with me, mind, that even with their ways, I don't always think of it. But you must be easy on her."

"I will be," said Louisa-Margaretta, flashing her most brilliant smile.

Louisa-Margaretta had lied, because soon, she was fairly flying on the mare, ready to make up any ground that had been lost between her and the young man. But there would be no reason for Mr Crew to worry, because the horse was more than up to the task, she decided. The dog she had borrowed, however, was much slower. At one point, once she was well into the woods, Louisa-Margaretta admitted she would have to simply stop and wait for the poor little dog to catch up. She could not track William alone.

With the help of the old hunting dog, she was sure she was getting close. As they picked their way through the forest, she became so lost in her thoughts that she hardly noticed they were retracing their steps. Apparently, William truly did wander, perhaps without much of an aim in his mind.

She wished she could have been as carefree.

## 24

Louisa-Margaretta, her feet dangling from a tree, had her first jolt of amusement when she saw her brother.

"Percival!" she called. "Come and join us! William would like to stay here all day, so I shall require some company."

She would also require some sort of refreshment, at least bread and water. But as long as she could persuade Peggy to guard the base of the gnarled tree while she went back to the home for a brief interlude, she was quite sure she would be able to climb back up and outlast the man easily. They were fortunate the tree was near the path that was a shortcut to the village, as Peggy had happened to be passing.

"I am sure Mr, er, William can manage without company, and you can climb down at this instant, Louisa-Margaretta," her brother said. Not knowing William's last name, he stumbled over how to refer to the young man, who was currently picking minuscule pieces of bark off the trunk. Louisa-Margaretta knew that even away from the home, he was referred to simply as Wandering William, and she could not have thought of a more apt title for him.

"Scolding does not suit you," she said to Percival, pretending to be perturbed. "We were always being scolded together, remember? Come join me."

"I would like to speak with Mrs Haddington first," he said, the formality no doubt for William's benefit.

"Yes, Mr Haddington?" asked Peggy archly, her back still against the tree trunk. "As you can see, we are rather occupied, so perhaps you had better speak quickly."

"Then I shall. I can be a man of few words, if you press me. Even though it is not my natural inclination."

Louisa-Margaretta plucked a leaf from her branch, laughing. "Percival, with all those words, you still have not begun to come to the point. Let me guess. You are going into the army again, and they are sending you straight to France. Only, you need to know how to describe exactly the wine you want, which, considering the state of your French, will not be easy."

"This concerns you, too, Louisa-Margaretta. You both need to come with me. This instant."

Louisa-Margaretta gave a theatrical gasp. "But what about our William? It would hardly be sporting to leave him in this tree all alone!"

She twinkled up at the young man, who only looked away.

"It is not safe here," continued Percival with a frown. "Neither of you told me there was a man who stated the doctor ought to suffer just before the murder. Apparently, his words were so loud they could be heard across the fields. All the villagers are saying the only reason he has not been locked away for the murder is that he is mad and locked away here as it is."

"Really, Percival," said Peggy, putting a hand on his arm. "You ought not to speak that way in front of William."

He put a hand on hers, and she met his eyes then drew away.

"You ought not to," she said again.

"We both know the man you speak of, dear brother. Archibald Finch is all boldness and not a great deal of activity. Would he really break away from his room to commit a murder only to come back to the building he escaped from and fall asleep, somehow repairing all the locks before he did so? It is hardly the work of a menace."

"These Lambs," said Percival. "They are putting you both in danger along with every man, woman, and child who is here. They ought to bear the consequences themselves."

"Peggy," said Louisa-Margaretta. "Please stay with the tree. I can stand no more of this."

She swung down, taking pleasure in the pain it would cause her brother. Though he had been eager enough to follow in her schemes when they were both much younger, lately, he seemed to recognise that his spinster sister would not be the toast of London society if it was found that she had gone climbing trees in pursuit of a madman.

"William is not safe either," Percival told her once her feet touched the ground. "The whole village is talking about how he was out that night. Whoever was supposed to be watching for him was clearly lax in their duties."

That time, Peggy flushed. "How dare you?"

"How dare I protect the two women dearest to me?"

Percival's gaze softened, but Peggy stepped away.

"This place has given me life," she said. "Purpose, breath, some measure of faith that God had not truly abandoned me. And you are so wild as to suggest that the Lambs are doing wrong, intentionally, to the people they have given everything to help?"

Louisa-Margaretta raised an eyebrow. She could not have said it better, and she enjoyed seeing Peggy's fighting spirit again. When Percival had first returned, she wondered whether her sister-in-law could rise to the challenge of avoiding society and her absent husband, but it appeared those worries were not well-founded.

"You may leave," said Peggy. "And, Louisa-Margaretta, you may go have a good meal, for I know that is why you came down. Kiss your foolish brother and have some food. I will stay with our William."

## 25

Louisa-Margaretta still had not succeeded in her aim, though Mr Crew had come to get his horse and dog. William remained up in the tree even late in the day.

But upon hearing a commotion not a hundred yards away, Louisa-Margaretta realised that if she did not come down from the lower branches, she would be giving up the opportunity to join a rather glorious picnic.

A party of ladies had gathered with a great deal of food. The offering was ample but simple, as was so often the case in the home. Louisa-Margaretta had to admit the idea was rather brilliant, at least for those ladies who would be able to join such a gathering without running off. Judith and Mercy were both there, with Judith watching Mercy closely. Peggy, who had left Louisa-Margaretta hours ago, was standing next to Judith, making some sort of impassioned plea.

Louisa-Margaretta had to get quite close to them before she was able to hear the conversation, though neither of them acknowledged her.

"It was a fair point," Peggy said. "Percival knows the harm gossip can do to a reputation, as do I."

Judith's face was pinched. "Then I wonder why you would indulge in gossip," she said. "Especially when it could harm the reputation of so many."

For a moment, Louisa-Margaretta started. *Has anything become known of my moments alone with Mr Fortescue?* Even if Federica had guessed, Louisa-Margaretta could hardly imagine such a betrayal. No, any gossip must have come only from Mr Fortescue himself. But she wondered how he could boast of a minor conquest while leaving out so many pertinent details—his grief, his tears, which Louisa-Margaretta believed were real, and his urgent belief that his brother had been murdered. She knew that he had not made that knowledge public, but he had plainly been tortured by his certainty.

She took a minute to contemplate Mr Fortescue's behavior. From what she understood, the two brothers had never been close, and they had truly fallen out some years ago after the doctor's scandalous behavior with the young woman he later married. Though, of course, the marriage had not quite been enough to quell the disapproval that was widespread once his behavior became public. Society, she mused, would always allow young men their seedy moments with young women of different classes. But when it came to a young woman who was both the daughter of a gentleman and considered virtuous or had suddenly fallen from virtue, the judgement was quite different.

But Peggy's next statement set her at ease. "Percival believes it is possible," she said. "And really, Judith, who else would have wished the doctor dead if not one of us? The villagers hardly knew him, and he had shunned London society for many years. It is not likely that a murderer simply happened upon his cottage, taking nothing."

Judith shook her head, weary. "I cannot agree with you," she said. "But I can tell you that you are here to mind the women, and I am here to care for Mercy."

"Not to find a killer, even though that seems to be your quaint little amusement?" Peggy was looking at both of them. "I thought the two of you loved searching for justice."

"What I meant," said Judith, her voice still quiet, "was that you really ought to talk to Margaret."

Louisa-Margaretta had no interest in taking part in such a conversation, but she greatly wished to hear the grand female superintendent's response to Percival's sordid accusations against William, Archibald, or some unknown person in their number. She went up to Bathsheba, who was sitting only a few feet from her mother, staring into the distance as Margaret spoke to her.

"One really must make the effort," Margaret was saying. "This time, it is not a trouble that thou mayest escape by traveling."

She broke off as Louisa-Margaretta sat down close to Bathsheba and greeted her. Judith greeted Margaret.

Joyce was sitting with an infant on each knee, but she rushed over when she saw Bathsheba drooping over like a wilted flower.

"Here, take her, my little goose," she said. "I may be able to feed two, but I cannot carry more than one."

Louisa-Margaretta was afraid Bathsheba would suffocate the little thing. Instead, she touched her lips to the baby's head, seeming to drink in the scent, and held her gently. She nodded her thanks.

"It will all come right in the end, lamb," said Joyce. "The babies are loved, just like everyone else who is here, and that can be the end of it. Much better that than having them far away, even if this all feels a bit strange to some."

Louisa-Margaretta tried to keep her attention from wandering. In fact, it all seemed extraordinarily strange to her. *Why not simply give both of the infants to Joyce Garvey at her own home and be done with it?* She kept looking around, wondering if someone would hurt one of them.

But the ladies, when they had a chance to hold one child or another, were gentle. Clarinda had just walked over to Bathsheba and asked to hold the older one, though Bathsheba shook her head. Joyce surrendered her charge without hesitation.

"Many arms, many hands. That's what good for a little one," she said pointedly in what seemed to be a rebuke to Bathsheba. "The babies are better for it. Take it from me."

Louisa-Margaretta cleared her throat. "Is there still no news of the families who left them?" she asked Margaret.

Margaret looked about. Bathsheba and Joyce were making faces at the baby Bathsheba was holding, and one of the older ladies was singing a soft lullaby. Nobody was listening to Louisa-Margaretta.

"Louisa-Margaretta," she said slowly, as if each syllable of the name were a punishment. "We do not question too deeply. These children are a gift from God, and it must be our mission to care for them."

"But surely we must find out who left them. What if they know something of the doctor's murder?"

As if Margaret had been struck by lightning, she wavered, then her face tightened with resolve. "That is slanderous talk. I took thee in because of thy sister-in-law, our dear Peggy. But, Louisa-Margaretta, do not mistake me. If I hear more gossip of this kind, I will send thee away. Immediately."

Louisa-Margaretta opened her mouth to object, but she could see Margaret was quite serious.

"Very well," she said. "I cannot promise to stop my brother from gossiping. But you'll hear no more from me."

She walked away with the disquieting sense of both being scolded and having done wrong. It was unfamiliar and uncomfortable, like a stone in her shoe.

Not until much later did she remember that Margaret had been even more disquieted by the talk of murder than she had and wondered what to make of the knowledge.

**26**

———

Judith and Louisa-Margaretta were finally able to speak as the ladies were having their pudding. Bathsheba had been shepherded over to the building by her mother and was looking positively mutinous as she scraped around bits of food. Whatever quarrel had begun earlier in the day had not ended, then. Peggy's face was drawn and pale. But the pudding was rather exceptional, and as there were enough ladies about to mind the assembled parties, Judith begged Louisa-Margaretta's assistance on a small matter of repairing a seam. They hurried on their way up to the room Judith shared with Mercy.

"Peggy looked rather suspicious when you spoke of that seam," said Louisa-Margaretta. "She knows I cannot sew worth anything."

"I hope she won't give us away."

Louisa-Margaretta shrugged. The halls were quiet, but they could never quite be sure that nobody was listening, so she lowered her voice, saying, "What young lady would not wish to escape that company, I wonder. It seemed Marla was about ready to fling a bite of parsnip at me. Only Margaret's stare stopped her. My, but that woman is a dragon today. Like Mama gets if someone breaks her rules about Lenten fasting."

Judith gave a timid smile. "I would have broken your mother's rules, I am certain, had I only known where to find more food."

"Well, I am sure you would have had a difficult time. Every year, I have to think of a new way to outwit her or starve trying."

"Every year except this past one."

They were on the last staircase, which was narrow. Judith thought again of Louisa-Margaretta's London life. Before the two of them had met, she realised, their lives had not been entirely different. Though Judith lived in the humblest rented accommodations, she and Louisa-Margaretta were both surrounded by siblings and family most of their days. Their lives were determined by their parents, most especially by their mothers, and it was expected that in due course, they would marry tolerably well. True, for Louisa-Margaretta, a tolerably good marriage might have been to a man who was both rich and titled, and for Judith, simply to a gentleman who could appreciate that she brought breeding and education without a good deal of money. Still, many of the assumptions about their future were much the same.

But Peggy's madness had changed the course for both of them. It had made Louisa-Margaretta eager to escape her beloved parents, whom she blamed for all sorts of evils, Peggy's illness among them. Louisa-Margaretta had decided, for the first time in her life, that the fact of being a spinster dependent on her parents was troublesome enough to make even the most mercenary of marriages into an offer she really ought to consider. Judith had been shocked when Louisa-Margaretta told her of her change of heart.

For Judith, what had happened to Peggy reminded her of her own failure. She had not helped the other woman early enough, and around that time, she had also let down many other individuals who depended on her. She needed to repent, to be less of the world and more devoted to ministering to its unfortunates. What was more, everything that had passed between Peggy and Percival Haddington had convinced her that marriage was rather dangerous. The isolation and celibacy of the home was exactly what she wished for—or what she'd believed she wished for when she first made the decision to stay.

"Do you miss London?" Judith could not help asking once they'd reached her room.

It should have been a familiar feeling, retreating with the young woman who had once been one of her closest friends to what they hoped was a quiet space. But instead, she felt only uncomfortable. Louisa-Margaretta had other friends in London, older friends who were more sophisticated, and she imagined most of their conversations involved discussions of French fashions and bites of barely imaginable delicacies. And of course, many of the gatherings involved single men, even unscrupulous ones such as Mr Fortescue.

Louisa-Margaretta frowned. "I needed to escape when I did. No, I suppose I do not miss it."

Judith could feel the weight of what was unsaid. "Yet?"

"I miss what I wished London could give me. What I expected of the ton and failed to receive, of course."

"And the company?"

Judith nearly blushed. That was as close as she could get to alluding to Mr Fortescue. Louisa-Margaretta's eyes, as shrewd as ever, missed nothing and met Judith's in the light of the fading sunset.

"If you are asking about a certain gentleman, I am not sure I miss him. But I did feel deeply for him. I cannot deny that. I know what it is to lose a brother."

For a moment, neither of them spoke, examining their shared memories and their separate ones. Judith had only fragmented memories of the babies who had been lost between Miriam's birth and her three healthy, much younger brothers, but her parents had always spoken of them often. She knew the names of the children and how well they had been loved. She had to imagine that Louisa-Margaretta's experience, of a brother not quite lost but very nearly, must have been terrifying. And perhaps running off to the haut ton, with its balls and its reliance on social scandal, could have been the only thing she could bear after the ordeal.

For the first time, she was bold enough to ask her friend about it. "Your brother says you are not happy."

"My mother and your father, I daresay, would tell us there are things more important than worldly happiness."

Judith gave a small smile. "Yes, but they both have rather easy temperaments and are quite often happy."

"I can tell you, then, what is making me unhappy. It is that a man has been murdered, and we are none of us safe. Yet we bow down to Margaret and will not look for the murderer, who is almost certainly here."

Judith sighed. "You have to remember… well, you can't remember. You were never here before." She held up a hand. "I am not blaming you, Louisa-Margaretta. Ah, what a delight, to say *you* instead of *thee* again! But the doctor's behavior was inexcusable. I am sure he has been forgiven by our creator, but I am also quite sure nobody else here would have the temerity to treat others as he did."

"You persist, then, in saying he treated others poorly, not just with a sort of brusque efficiency?"

"You must believe me. He treated nearly everyone, especially women, as unworthy of his consideration, let alone his respect."

Louisa-Margaretta moved closer to Judith, though she raised her voice, giving her the curious impression that the room itself was shrinking.

"Come, Judith. Leave your scruples. Whatever else you may think, I know you wonder about the culprit just as much as I do. And I think we can tell from my reception here that I cannot solve it on my own. Nobody will confide in me."

"Louisa-Margaretta, you are too hasty. It was months before anyone trusted me either. You see, the women who come to us—"

"Yes, yes, I am sure it is all rather sad, only we haven't got that sort of time."

Judith smiled gently. "Because of your obligations in London? Truly, Louisa-Margaretta, I do not agree wholeheartedly with Margaret, but I do know that if we give in to these rumors of murder, people like Peggy might never be able to come here again. They would all be sent to Bethlem to lose toes and be treated as wild beasts."

"And you would not be able to stay either," said Louisa-Margaretta. "Is that where your objection lies?"

Her accusation of selfishness stung, and Judith moved away, going in search of her sewing box. It was locked away in case Mercy had a fit. Perhaps someone would come up and wonder why they plainly did not intend to do any work.

When Judith still did not answer, Louisa-Margaretta

gave an exasperated sigh. "Very well. You would rather spend all your years here. Having been a witness to my friend Federica's state of wedded bliss, I cannot promise the outside world has anything better to offer. But Judith, only think what it would mean if we did nothing and the murderer killed someone else."

Judith unlocked her trunk slowly. "Really, how sordid!"

"No, it is only the logical progression that a killer would move through, one we have certainly seen in the past. After a second murder, there would be no doubt, and your place here might vanish in a moment."

Judith took out a needle and thread but did not move them. She was thinking.

Perhaps it was that she had been working in the home for over a year or that she had seen Mercy in what to outsiders seemed to be absolutely uncontrollable rages. Nothing about William that could frighten her. Archibald, though, at times, sent chills through her when he yelled enough for anyone within a mile to hear. Something about those sounds was unnatural. And he had escaped. It was not the word they were supposed to use, but she knew that she was not the only person, lady or gentleman, who wondered what exactly he had done that night.

It had not occurred to her that he might attempt to do such a thing again.

She turned. "All right. I will discover what I can. But I will need to request something very particular from you."

Louisa-Margaretta beamed the way she always had as a spoiled child when the red face and fountains of tears she summoned up were rewarded with a treat. "As long as it does not involve sewing, I am quite sure I can grant your request."

## 27

The next day, Louisa-Margaretta was working in the garden.

She wondered, as Margaret scolded her once again for pulling up something that was supposed to be a vegetable, how she had stooped so low as to kneel in the dirt, patting about, to guard her food against weeds. She seemed to be there for the amusement of others. Even Clarinda was laughing, her cheeks red beneath her bonnet.

At least the weather was fair. And some of the women did seem a little different when they got their hands in the soil. Bathsheba was more animated, though she did seem to need a little bit more rest than the others. Louisa-Margaretta found it rather amusing that Bathsheba's parents coddled her. In that way, they were no different from her parents. Though Bathsheba was forced to learn how to cook, clean, and take care of the women who were at the home, her parents seemed more amused than upset that she did none of it well. The only task she performed naturally was caring for the infants, and even then, she clearly favored the older one.

*Constance,* she remembered. That was supposed to be the name. And the younger one was going to be Charity or something like that. Quakers had their own strange ways of naming children. They did not recognise a man in a cassock with holy water and seemed instead to wish all of their number to name the child at once. There had been some very dull talk last time she was with the superintendents of when and how that would happen, but everything seemed to be suspended after the doctor's death.

Louisa-Margaretta liked the smaller, uglier child better than fair Constance, though she was not particularly eager to see or hold either of them. In her mind, that was not work for a mother, even, but for a wet nurse like Joyce. But Louisa-Margaretta, who had always been a beautiful child and knew herself to be a beautiful woman, was feeling for the first time what it was to be unattractive and unwanted. While others begged to sit next to Peggy at table, or to go up to visit Judith during her quiet moments with Mercy, they showed none of the same affection for Louisa-Margaretta.

"Tell me this isn't a plant," she said to the silent Marla, "or I shall have to admit defeat. My gifts are in the realm of eating, not gardening."

Marla raised her eyebrows. "They're all plants," she said shortly.

Louisa-Margaretta repressed a sigh. "A weed, then. Or whatever one is meant to call them. I'm not sure what the difference is when they can all be eaten anyway. My father used to have the most tedious stories about eating soups made from weeds as a little boy."

That got a response, which surprised her. "He wasn't born rich, then, thy father?"

"No, of course. Otherwise, he would never have become so rich."

"How?" asked Marla.

Louisa-Margaretta was surprised to hear that she was still talking.

"My mother was born rich, and she has no interest in money. I would as soon sit on a pincushion as go a season without new gowns, but I have no head for business and no desire to earn my keep. With my father, no amount of riches will ever be enough. He was born wanting to better his situation, and so he shall remain."

"A hard man, then?"

"Oh, not at all. Not with me. He is as gentle as a lamb at home. I am sure you can see that he spoils his children."

Marla gave a gruff laugh. "Yes."

"Only, he cannot stop working, and no matter what he buys, he will always end up with more business and not less. My mother goes on about avarice, but she knows as well as anyone that this is simply how his mind works. I should ask him to buy us another gardener, then we won't have to stoop in the dirt in this fashion."

"It wouldn't do any good," said Lucy, who had been working nearby. "Margaret feels that both the sun and the work will do us good."

"The sun certainly will not," said Louisa-Margaretta, hoping that there was enough dirt on her hands to protect them from looking at all tan. They had special gloves they were supposed to use for that purpose, of course, but her pair had been so uncomfortable that she'd ripped them off after hardly a moment.

"I'm not sure that the work will either," said Lucy. "But I suppose it is something for the mind. Last night, I did not sleep well, and now I feel as if I could run to my bed and close my eyes this very moment."

Louisa-Margaretta closed her own eyes, sitting back on her heels to savor such a thought.

"Louisa-Margaretta" came Margaret's voice.

"It was only the barest moment of rest," she snapped. "I work for six moments then rest for a seventh. Quite Biblical, I can assure you."

"I assure *thee*," she corrected gently. "There is a visitor in my parlor. Thy can have another moment of rest."

**28**

———

"I've spoken to everyone, Percival," said Louisa-Margaretta as she went to the doorway. "Nobody is interested in this murder but me, so if you think it will force Peggy's hand, I'm afraid you're quite mistaken."

Mr Fortescue raised his eyebrows. "You take an interest in my brother's murder, then? Why, that is rather singular."

Before she could respond, she heard Margaret enter the house, and soon, the four of them were together. Percival, Louisa-Margaretta, Mr Fortescue, and Margaret made for an odd party indeed. And when Percival left in a huff, it left only the two women and their strange visitor.

"May I offer thee some tea?" Margaret asked only Mr Fortescue. "We also have some of the cake from last night. In spite of the taste, it was so large that we could not finish it. But then, I am sure you heard from your brother about how much we are spending on sugar. I am afraid it is one of our few indulgences."

Mr Fortescue was all charm, as usual. "I would love the opportunity to have some of both," he said, grinning at her. "I am glad my brother got to enjoy them for so long."

Margaret provided refreshments, and they made simple conversation about the weather until she was called away to see to one of the other visitors.

"Well," said Mr Fortescue, "I thought your Margaret would never leave us. Imagine my disappointment when she insisted on having a cup of tea! I suppose my reputation has followed me out into this little hamlet. I should not be surprised."

He moved over to sit next to Louisa-Margaretta. "Now, darling," he said. "Where did we leave off in London?"

"We left off here," she said, trying to force coldness into her trembling voice. "You said that your brother was murdered. And I decided to find the murderer."

He had been reaching for her hand, but that was enough to stop him and make him sit straighter. "What? You, find the murderer?"

"To bring you peace of mind," she said haughtily. *And to escape you,* she added mentally, hoping he would not try to touch her. For if he made an attempt, she knew she might well abandon her pretense of being a reformed young lady.

"Peace of mind," he said. "Well, I cannot have that. Not while my brother's murderer walks free, nor while you walk free, rejecting all my offers and ignoring my letters."

"I read your letter," she said. "It did offer some information. I will use that as I search for the killer."

"You sound quite sure you will find him."

"Him or her. The murderer may well be a woman."

He laughed, putting an arm across the back of her chair so that it was very nearly touching her, and she could feel the warmth of his breath as he leaned in.

"A woman, to kill a young and strong man in this way? Who would believe such a thing?"

"I would."

"You would kill a young man, or you would believe another had done it?"

"Either. Both." She met his gaze, looking at him steadily. "Were I sufficiently provoked, that is."

He pulled her off the chair and placed her in his lap all in one swift movement, then he was kissing her, and she was completely in thrall. It was less that she knew their actions were forbidden and more that her genuine desire for Mr Fortescue and his body was keeping her from objecting.

Louisa-Margaretta heard Bathsheba just in time and was able to sit back down in her chair as the young woman came in.

"Mama said there was more cake. I'm sorry. I am starving, and the garden was quite hot."

Noticing Mr Fortescue, she started. She blinked in surprise but did not apologise, which seemed rather strange to Louisa-Margaretta.

"I will take some of this," she said softly. "Louisa-Margaretta, please forgive me."

"Consider yourself forgiven," said Mr Fortescue, and it was not lost on Louisa-Margaretta that he stared at her with both desire and amusement in his eyes.

Bathsheba only shook her head, leaving the room.

Mr Fortescue smiled, leaning back in his chair. "I had hoped for yet more time with you," he said. "Perhaps we can meet."

She could not accuse him of forgetting himself, as she had forgotten herself as well.

"You will not have any more time with me, and I'll thank you to not to slander me to others," she said, wishing she had heeded the warnings of the haut ton. He was a man who wished not only to sully her reputation but to make her disgrace public as well. Yet she had been taken in by him again, thanks to nothing better than his looks.

"You ought to go," she said. "The road to town will not be safe in the dark."

He smiled. "It is not a long one." He made no attempt to stray from his position in what had been her chair.

She sat angrily on the sofa, where he had once been. "I must return to the garden."

"To this talk of the murder," he said. "You seem to think I will not be able to find the culprit."

"You won't."

"The faith you have in me is rather touching."

He was murmuring. Bathsheba was speaking animatedly, though she had moved into a different room. Louisa-Margaretta moved her chair two feet to the left, ensuring she was in full view of anyone who might pass the open doorway, including Bathsheba. Whatever Mr Fortescue's boasts might be, he would not touch her there if he wanted to continue his access to the little community.

And it was that access that formed the basis of Louisa-Margaretta's idea.

"I will find the murderer for you," she said. "And in return, you will never seek me out or speak to me again. What is more, you will not gossip about me again."

"And if you do not find the murderer?" he asked. "I must stand to benefit from this arrangement if I am to agree."

"What would you have me do?"

He gave a wide smile. "Why, marry me, of course."

## 29

The next day was Sunday—visiting day, or what passed for it. Of course, the superintendents had allowed the visit from Mr Fortescue the previous day. That, Louisa-Margaretta suspected, was more from Margaret's wish to console the grieving man than from any actual rule.

If only she knew what he had actually come for, she would not feel guilty. He had stayed at the little inn in the next village instead of returning to town, claiming the arrangements were not complete.

At least, that was what he said to Percival and Louisa-Margaretta as they encountered him outside the church. He was plainly not a churchgoing man, and Louisa-Margaretta wondered how he had known when to stand and when to sit. She was determined not to look at him the entire service and succeeded only because she and Percival had arrived early enough to sit closer to the front. Judith always went if she could be spared, but Louisa-Margaretta had accompanied her for the first time to beg her brother's presence.

It was rather awkward, of course, since she could not give a true reason.

"Percival," she said, "We would all like to see you. And if Judith and I are going to help your case with Peggy, we need to present you as a reasonable choice, one who might tempt even a very cautious woman."

"Am I a choice to tempt a cautious woman, then? Singular! I rather thought I was a devoted husband, asking my wife to live under my roof again."

Judith was already blushing, but she was not silent. "You can, perhaps, form your own opinion of the home," she murmured. "Louisa-Margaretta has always held that instinct is just as important as facts."

"My instinct," said Percival a bit too loudly, "is that my wife should leave, and were both of you admirably independent young ladies to join her in her removal from that place, I should be most obliged."

A reply was prevented by the beginning of the service. Louisa-Margaretta was smarting, but she could not think of a way to tell her brother that she needed him by her side. Mr Fortescue would be trying to steal moments alone with her, and he respected nothing and nobody. But Percival was familiar with his true character and would not be susceptible to Mr Fortescue's charms. He would not allow them a moment alone.

Judith's reply was prevented by her immutable status as a rector's daughter. She was silent throughout the service, prayerful, and if occasionally, her eyes did stray to Louisa-Margaretta in a moment where the passage being discussed pertained to their situation, she could surely be forgiven for such a minor lapse.

"Dearly beloved, avenge not yourselves, but rather give place unto wrath: for it is written, Vengeance is mine; I will repay, saith the Lord," droned the curate, and Judith saw even Percival take note.

Apart from that rather dramatic passage, the curate was dreadfully dull, and they all had an uncommon air of thanksgiving as they left the small place to file into the open air. That was, of course, rather short-lived.

"Mr Percival Haddington, Miss Haddington," said Mr Fortescue. "What a wonderful surprise, seeing you here. Might I ask for an introduction to your young friend?"

Percival's eyes narrowed, but he could not politely refuse it. He introduced Judith by name, but when there was a pause in which he might usually have said something about their connection or how she came to be in that particular village, he did not provide any information.

"I am sure we can walk together," said Mr Fortescue. "Alas, I must continue setting my brother's affairs in order, so I believe our destination is the same."

Judith murmured condolences, and Louisa-Margaretta nodded.

"I was very sorry to hear about your brother," said Percival.

"As was I," said Mr Fortescue, and Louisa-Margaretta caught the first flash of sincerity in his speech. She wondered if others noticed it. "Perhaps we did not live in a similar fashion, but there are so many people about, and few who are genuinely a part of one's family. And for the two of us, who look unlike most Londoners, that was particularly so."

Percival blushed at the acknowledgement of the difference, and Judith still said nothing. But Louisa-Margaretta recognised an opportunity.

"Did you look very like your brother, then, if I might

ask? I have never seen his portrait, though of course he was much loved and well-thought-of at the home."

Louisa-Margaretta had clenched her hands as she said it, determined that her tone of voice should be natural. She had decided she would not solve the murder to oblige Mr Fortescue but to save Judith's place in the home. Ever since she had mentioned the threat to her friend's livelihood, poor Judith had not been in good spirits.

The charm returned, and Mr Fortescue's grin was just a bit more wolfish than what might have been considered strictly polite. "As men, no, not particularly. But as children, we were very like. Even born with great patches of blue on our backs, which is common enough in the Orient, though not so much here when the infants have milky skin."

"There are two foundlings now at the home," said Judith. "Mr Haddington, I believe you had expressed interest in seeing them. They are very charming babies."

"Indeed," said Louisa-Margaretta with rather too much feeling. "They are lovely. Judith and I are going to help take care of them while you go about your business. I have a feeling we may find my sister-in-law there as well."

"Peggy always did dote on the little ones," said Percival thoughtfully. "It does not surprise me that she should wish to see them."

"Foundlings, you say?" asked Mr Fortescue. "I've heard that rumor, to be sure, but I thought they must certainly be the children of ladies at the home. Perhaps it was not delicate to acknowledge such a thing. Do the two sides mix much, then, the male prisoners with the women?"

"I say, Fortescue," said Percival, but before he could reprimand him, Louisa-Margaretta got there.

"They are none of them *prisoners*," she said firmly. "And no, the two sides seldom see each other socially. For meals in the superintendents' home, yes, on certain occasions. Otherwise, we are in separate parts of the building, and each side knows very little of what happens on the other."

"But I am sure you must hear and see plenty of the worst men," pressed Mr Fortescue.

To Louisa-Margaretta's relief, he did not pursue his filthy implication about the women who lived at the home. Though to be sure, it was also a rather absurd one. If any of them had actually given birth to a child, there would be no way to keep it secret, not with a dozen other women about and especially when many of those women did not feel bound by the rules of propriety.

"We do not think in terms of 'better' and 'worse,'" Judith said gently.

Mr Fortescue continued as if she had not spoken. "This William, I hear all about him. Seems he goes about the village, helping himself to whatever he likes!"

"He has eaten fruit in the summer," said Judith rather less quietly. "And only when he was nearly starving because he was out so long. We are able to see to it that he stays closer now."

"Ah, well, I am sure that is a relief," said Mr Fortescue with such an unpleasant tone that Percival stepped in.

"Sir," he said. "We are nearly arrived, and if you are going to pay a social call on these ladies and on my wife, I must suggest that you moderate your views."

Mr Fortescue gave him a sweeping bow. "Yes, of course."

"Otherwise," said Louisa-Margaretta, "perhaps we can join Joyce in her chambers. It wouldn't be proper for a gentleman, of course, but the two of you can visit together."

Both gave her looks of such horror that she almost smiled, and Mr Fortescue's grin turned into a sheepish expression.

"Please, Miss Haddington," he said. "If I offended you, I am very sorry."

She did not miss that his apology started with a conditional statement. But he looked so very lovely as he said it, the unpleasant expression in his face transformed into one of true doubt and apology, that she felt a small thrill as she turned to show them to the superintendents' home.

"This way, then."

**30**

---

They had chosen a good day to see the babies. Their nurse allowed it, with some persuasion, but she insisted on keeping the children outside in the fresh air.

Both babies were in fine form, with Constance gurgling and the other little one reaching out to touch her adopted aunties. Joyce's arms were soon empty as Peggy held the smaller baby, and Judith struggled to contain the surprisingly strong Constance.

Judith saw that Louisa-Margaretta was edging closer to Peggy as if she were afraid, which was most peculiar.

"What is this little one's name?" asked Louisa-Margaretta, touching the baby's head softly.

"Her name is Charity," said Peggy.

Joyce harrumphed. "Ought to have proper names, these little ones. Can't think why they are all waiting. I'm going to have words with the master and mistress of this house if they wait any longer. It isn't right, poor things."

"I believe that Quakers have different customs when it comes to baptism," said Judith quickly, looking into

Constance's little face. She was so much in the habit of not talking about parties when they were present that part of her wondered whether the little mite would understand and be offended. "Don't mind us, Constance," she said in a lower voice, but the child only squirmed.

"I'll take her again," said Joyce. "Not an easy one, either of them. But the fresh air keeps them quiet, mostly."

She moved closer to Peggy, and the two of them soon fell into a hushed conference about the little one's features as the nurse changed the tiny baby's underclothes with brisk efficiency. Louisa-Margaretta did not pretend to have any interest in the conversation.

Percival, meanwhile, was asking Judith about the way the place worked. He had tried to speak to Peggy when she first came out, but she dismissed him.

"Where is everyone when you have Sunday off, then?" he asked. "Just allowed to run free or locked in?"

Judith winced. "Some of our guests usually accompany us to church, but at the moment, all of them are Quakers, and they have gone to their own meeting."

She heard the murmuring from the rest of the ladies and wished she could join in, no matter how dull the conversation. "Such dark hair for her skin." "Looks almost like a bruise, only it isn't." And Louisa-Margaretta's "Oh, how extraordinary" floated over to her. They would be much better than Percival's inquisition.

"And nobody is locked in?" asked Percival.

"There is a sort of rotation to care for those who do not wish to attend. Today, I believe Mercy is attending the meeting, and Bathsheba is with any of the ladies who did not choose to go. None of them are compelled to worship."

"Bathsheba drew the short straw, then, I suppose?"

"She asked to stay," said Judith, looking about.

Bathsheba was the only person they could have called over for company, and lately, she was often to be found with Joyce, shirking all her other duties. But it appeared she was currently playing the part of a dutiful daughter.

"And for the men? That Archie fellow seems a bit of a character. I hope you've got good locks for him."

"Someone will be with him if he is not at their meeting. We do not visit the men's section, so I am less familiar with their arrangements."

"I, for one, would like to learn more about them," said Mr Fortescue, rising to his feet. "Miss Haddington, perhaps you will accompany me?"

Percival also rose. "I am sure that will not be necessary," he said, glaring at the man. "My sister is needed here."

"Two babies and four grown women? Come, man, I am sure she can be spared."

Louisa-Margaretta was touching Joyce's arm as if all her customary speeches had deserted her.

"She is needed here," said the nurse. "And unless Mr Haddington wants to go, you'll need to find the place yourself. With only two buildings in the whole place, begging your pardon, it can't be so hard for an educated gentleman."

She had a knack for saying "begging your pardon" with just enough iron in her tone to convey that she was not going to ask for anyone's pardon, much less beg.

"I am sure it will not," said Percival, smiling as he sat back down.

"Well," said Mr Fortescue, "perhaps, as the whole group is remaining here..." And he took a seat directly next to Louisa-Margaretta.

Judith, who had been watching the whole tableau silently, suddenly saw her role.

"Louisa-Margaretta," she said. "You should come with

me. We will go visit Bathsheba. And we can direct Mr Fortescue to the proper door on our way."

Mr Fortescue did not look particularly delighted, but he was as polite as he could be.

"Miss Haddington, you are tired," he said as they started off across the lawn toward the larger building. "Might I offer you my arm?"

When there was no response except in the form of Louisa-Margaretta moving closer to her friend again, Judith gave a wan smile.

"We are nearly there. Your door is that large one above the stairs. We must leave you here. We will go through the garden first. Must see that all is well since our hard work yesterday."

It was a lie, as neither of them had the least bit of interest in looking in on the vegetables, but it served its purpose for the moment.

"Well, thank you both for walking with me," he said. "Miss St Clair, Miss Haddington. I will rely upon a meeting with you later to discuss our plans for the future."

And with a smile that was not very gentlemanly, he sauntered off toward the building.

"What was he speaking of?" asked Judith as soon as they were alone. "Plans with such a man?"

Louisa-Margaretta shook her head. She took Judith's arm and drew her toward the woods. When they were amongst the trees, the silence that had gripped her for a good part of the morning seemed to finally release its hold.

"I have promised to marry him," she said. "That is, if we do not find the killer before he does."

Judith let out a gasp of horror. "But the doctor might have died a natural death! We do not even know for certain that there *is* a killer, let alone that we will find him!"

Louisa-Margaretta put her hand on one of the tree trunks then put her elegant shoe on the first branch. She had worn a resplendent gown that none of the Quaker ladies would have liked. With its lovely cerulean color and details of fine lace and delicate sleeves, it was exactly the opposite of plain dress. Judith was rather sad that she had not been able to show it to Mercy and wondered if it would be ripped to pieces by the tree.

"You do not think he died a natural death," said Louisa-Margaretta. "But as to our speed in finding the killer, it will depend on both of us."

"You will ruin your gown!" cried Judith.

"I know this tree well," said Louisa-Margaretta. "William knows how to choose a tree. You, however, will ruin your gown if you try to follow me."

Judith's lips were firmly set. She might think herself above such pursuits, and she was not nearly as tall or long-limbed as her friend, but she, too, had grown up with brothers. And she had a mother indulgent enough to warn her against falling out of trees but not against climbing them.

She would do it without shoes, however. She took off her shoes and stockings and began, with some difficulty, to follow her friend.

"That is nothing," she said, panting. "Perhaps we will find the murderer. But, Louisa-Margaretta, if you do not wish to marry Mr Fortescue, how on earth could you agree to such a thing?"

Louisa-Margaretta was already too high up for Judith to see. "I suppose he rather forced my hand."

"But you have spent a year and a half rejecting proposals from half the eligible men in London, not to mention many years before that," said Judith, blushing a bit as she revealed just how much she knew of the way her friend had been passing her days since they were parted. Judith had been quiet, in one of the two brick buildings very near them, doing hard work that most people would consider unimportant. Even those who had a friend or family member come to the home sometimes disliked visiting, considering the whole thing distasteful. Judith had thought that Louisa-Margaretta was one of those ladies, at least, before she realised that Peggy's condition was terrifying to Louisa-Margaretta, not simply bothersome.

"Well, I may have to accept this one. You see, he told me I could not force his hand on a different matter without offering something in return, and I rather agreed. It would not have been sporting, and moreover, he would never have agreed to it."

Judith pushed a branch back, but it sprang into place again, and she had to close her eyes while the leaves whipped into her mouth. Spitting, she asked, "I cannot understand a word, Louisa-Margaretta. What did you ask him for that could possibly be so important?"

"My freedom. I wish he would leave me alone and never see me again."

That was a mystery indeed.

"That he would leave you in peace?" asked Judith. "Louisa-Margaretta, you often ask that from other men. Demand it, even."

"I could not demand it from him."

Judith thought of one of the times when she had received unwanted though honorable attentions from a rather unappealing neighbor. "You always told me that your gun would be sufficient to dispatch any unwanted suitor."

Louisa-Margaretta gave a low laugh. "Yes, but in this case, I would not be able to bring myself to shoot. So there is not much point in that."

Judith could finally see her friend's feet, though the last two branches were more of a struggle for her, and when she joined Louisa-Margaretta, it was on an opposite branch where she could hug the trunk of the tree as if it were a dear friend.

"Louisa-Margaretta, are you saying you fancy this man?"

"I would never say that," said Louisa-Margaretta contemptuously. "I do not know that there is a good word for my feelings."

Judith looked out into the leaves then down at her gown. She had certainly damaged it, though she thought that patches might do very well. Since it was not nearly as fine as Louisa-Margaretta's, it would be much easier to repair.

"More than one word, then," said Judith gently.

"I am already afraid that if he asks me to marry him again, I might accept him," said Louisa-Margaretta. "Or worse, that I would consent to something dishonorable with him. An elopement. Or…"

Judith could read the scenarios she left out and frowned. "Though he is such a man? He treats the whole world abominably."

"He does," said Louisa-Margaretta thoughtfully. "But with me, there is genuine kindness, at least sometimes. It makes it difficult to remember what he really is."

"And you do not trust yourself to remember?"

"No," she said sadly. "Perhaps in happier times, I would have. But will I really be able to deny myself a companion for all eternity? If he were offering to take me away from a life full of joy, activity, and meaning, perhaps I could resist him. A life of love. But I have known only emptiness since I went to London, and he says he will banish all that. And it would be a good match, too, according to most."

"A terrible match, I would say."

"Well, then, help me find the killer again."

"I mean to help you! Only, we have a great deal of names and little to go on besides that."

Judith focused on one of the windows on the fourth story. They could see it quite well from William's tree.

"I believe we have a bit more to go on now."

Louisa-Margaretta could not keep herself from gasping. "Oh, Judith, surely not!"

Judith's gaze was steady. "I am very sorry to accuse anyone, but you can see it for yourself. Have you ever heard of an innocent thief?"

## 31

Judith and Louisa-Margaretta's conference was cut short when Peggy came running to the tree. They were already at the base, but they had stopped before going into the home. The meeting and the meal that followed must have ended, but they needed to discuss what they had seen.

"But truly," Louisa-Margaretta said as if she were talking to a child, "how much do you actually know about what is happening here?"

"It is all supposed to be fairly simple," said Judith. "But I wonder that it has grown from nothing. One superintendent, many subscribers, two or three guests. They did not acquire this building until they needed it, then they built more rooms. And the superintendents' home came later, of course."

"Quite a lovely and large home for them, I should think," said Louisa-Margaretta archly. "And how many guests are there? It is rather interesting when it seems that everyone here is mad, not just the people who pay for the privilege of admittance."

"Louisa-Margaretta," said Judith, "there could yet be a reasonable explanation."

"For such an act!" Louisa-Margaretta raised her eyebrows. "I am surprised at you, Judith. And you a rector's daughter—"

"Are the two of you going in?" asked Peggy. There were tears on her cheeks.

Judith rushed over to her, searching her pockets for a handkerchief. The one she found was crumpled and not particularly soft, but Peggy took it with thanks.

"Louisa-Margaretta, perhaps thou canst go in my stead."

Frowning, Louisa-Margaretta said, "I am not a 'thou.' What is the matter with you? Why can't you speak plainly?"

Peggy gave a small laugh. "I used to. But no matter. Many things have changed."

Louisa-Margaretta only shrugged. "I suppose I had better get to it, then. I will take your place, Peggy, for my sins. There are a great deal of ladies for me to offend before the afternoon is over."

She flounced into the building, clearly not as disturbed by what she had seen as Judith was. Judith wished they could continue their conversation, but she could not leave Peggy to cry alone.

"Peggy," said Judith, placing an arm across the woman's shoulders, "what has happened?"

She wondered briefly if perhaps nothing had happened. One thing she had learned at the home was that events in the memory could be every bit as painful as something that was happening that very day. For a great while, Peggy had only been tormented by the past, as their life in the home was simple and inoffensive. Judith had thought she was past it, but with Percival's visit, perhaps anything she had been holding in her heart had burst forth.

"It was lovely having my husband here," she said. "At least, after you got that horrid Mr Fortescue away from us. Percival and I were enjoying the children, and even Joyce said we were both uncommonly good with them. She said the superintendent is too gruff, Margaret too sad, and Bathsheba altogether taken away by her emotions."

"I am glad," said Judith without remarking on Peggy's choice to acknowledge that her husband still had a place in her life. "And Percival?"

"He is leaving the village and he won't give me a reason. Something about the visit today is forcing him away, just when I thought things would be different. And to think it must be all my fault! If only I had faith in someday wishing to return to a different life—but I thought I would be here forever, and so..."

She was openly weeping, and Judith was torn between comforting the woman who had once again become a friend and returning to her duties.

"Can I bring you something?" she asked. "I think you and Mr Haddington were so taken with the children that you were both neglecting the refreshments."

She only wept more. "I thought he was taken with the children. I thought, but it must have been an error. No, bring me nothing. A walk is as good a cure as any."

This last bit was said with some bitterness. It was a favorite saying of Margaret's. But the female superintendent, for all her kindness, never seemed to truly lose her temper. Judith wondered if she was best suited to take care of men and women who were truly out of sorts. She seldom seemed to experience even the smallest fit herself. Even Judith, who rarely cried, had lost hours or even days to fits of weeping every bit as violent as Peggy's. Margaret, she thought, must be the sort of woman who did not weep. It was not that she was without emotion but that there seemed to be walls around her heart.

"Peggy," said Judith, but her friend had hung her head low and was walking slowly away from the tree.

Judith turned to go back into the home. She would find Louisa-Margaretta, she decided. What they had witnessed from the tree must have some bearing on the doctor's murder. She simply could not see it yet.

**32**

—————

Margaret insisted that Peggy have a hot bath when she came in from the woods. She took Mercy under her wing, which was no easy feat, as Mercy had apparently been out of sorts ever since they returned that afternoon. She had been calm enough at the meeting and at the meal that followed, and Margaret insisted that everyone in attendance treat Mercy with particular care. But after they returned, she went to the superintendents' house, where she met all the visitors, and after that, she shrieked and moaned almost constantly.

Still, Margaret told Judith to go to Peggy. "She needs to speak to someone. And Louisa-Margaretta is having an easier time of things today."

"Meaning nobody has thrown anything at her yet?"

"I am quite sure that none of our guests would throw something at your dear friend Louisa-Margaretta."

"If they did," said Judith, "I am sure it would be justified."

All the same, she went to find Peggy, though it meant leaving Margaret caring for Mercy, which was sure to be difficult for anyone who could not play Bach. She wished she could see what was happening with Louisa-Margaretta and the rest of the ladies, but Peggy was having a hot bath, which spoke to the difficulties she was experiencing. That treatment was reserved for guests, usually, but it was typically quite effective.

"I forgot how lovely this is," said Peggy. "It is almost worth going mad for such a luxury."

Judith winced. "You know better than to use such a word, I am sure, Peggy."

"I do not dislike using the word." Peggy took a cake of soap in her hands and examined it as if it were a strange little animal she had never seen before. "It describes how I was feeling when I came. And how I am feeling today."

Judith frowned. Trusted individuals such as Peggy were to add hot water themselves, so she offered to help Peggy with the heavy jug and poured a little bit of water on her friend's shoulders.

"Perhaps it will look better soon," she said, though she knew that was not the right approach. "I am sorry. I do not mean to make light of your pain."

"Well, it is pain from different sources now," said Peggy. "Listen, Judith, will you go over and check on the children?"

Judith frowned. "The infants? The ones in the superintendents' home?"

"Yes."

She blinked, watching as Peggy looked at the soap again then looked up without touching it. "I do not feel they are safe, and they are defenseless, poor things, more so than the rest of us. Percival is blind. He worries for us and for his sister when he should really be thinking of those poor innocents."

Judith shifted. "I am not sure anyone is in danger,

Peggy," she said, though of course that was not entirely true, based on what she had seen earlier. "And I am going to have to go straight to Mercy. She is not well tonight."

"Send Louisa-Margaretta, then. If she is minding the ladies, they will be heartily sick of her by now."

"I'll tell her to look in on the children, but after your bath, perhaps you can go to her."

Peggy made to stand, but Judith shook her head. "Truly, you must wait. Margaret is not going to allow any of us to run off so quickly. But if Lucy will come up during the pudding and sit for a while, everyone will be in good spirits, and I am sure Louisa-Margaretta can get across the lawn."

"But she should go now," said Peggy, standing up, her face pink from heat and frustration.

"Peggy," said Judith firmly. "I understand that you have cares. Premonitions, even. But if I rush off to replace Louisa-Margaretta or if you give up a bath to do so, every single person is going to know that you suspect the infants will come to harm. Could this not place them in even greater danger?"

"I suppose." Peggy shivered but did not move.

Judith placed a hand on her naked shoulder. "Sit. I will go see to Mercy, and after everyone has eaten, you can send Louisa-Margaretta off. I am quite sure she will be more than ready to escape. But make sure you think of a reason for her going, or it will still look very odd."

"Very well," said Peggy, sitting back in the water. But she had worry etched all over her face.

She reminded Judith of their guests who, forgetting where they were, would say things like "I must go give my sons their tea" or "My daughter has a fever. Call a doctor right away." Strangely, she had the same manner as one of the young mothers.

## 33

"Returning this little lamb?" asked Louisa-Margaretta. "What a silly errand. I'm not even sure why you brought her here, Peggy. No, you can take it over yourself."

She thought her sister-in-law looked uncommonly ill. Even freshly scrubbed, Peggy looked cold and nervy. Perhaps she had gotten all the good she could out of the home, and any additional time would only make her believe she was mad. Indeed, Peggy was holding the child with such care that Louisa-Margaretta could hardly stand to see it.

"You won't hurt it, you know, if you hold it up," Louisa-Margaretta said, taking the baby from Peggy and resting its little face on her shoulder.

"You won't hurt *her*," said Peggy, her voice tremulous. "But perhaps you could deliver Charity to Joyce's arms yourself. She needs milk. She's been here for an hour already. Judith suggested that I go get her after my bath so she could say good night to all the ladies."

Louisa-Margaretta tried not to roll her eyes. Judith certainly made some very strange suggestions, and having different women run across the lawn so the infant could "say good night" to a room full of strangers was exceptionally odd.

She thought of what she had learned earlier. Perhaps she could bend the errand to her own purposes, even if she disagreed with the idea of running about with the little mite.

"We have to keep them safe," said Peggy. "All of the little ones."

"Why? Why would anyone want to hurt one of these children? They can't do a thing for themselves."

"That's why we must be careful with them," said Peggy. "How we can be certain they will be safe?"

Louisa-Margaretta wondered how to answer. And thinking it all over again, she wondered whether she did fully disagree with that idea of staying a bit more attentive to the infants. She and Judith had not been able to fully explain what they had seen. Maybe there was some sort of scheme afoot, involving two babies who had doubtless been placed on the steps of the home because it was the only place within a hundred miles that was truly open to all. *How would I feel if I neglected them simply because I had not made all the connections in time?*

"I'm sure they are safe with Joyce," she said, but she hesitated. The baby resting on her shoulder was troublesome but fragile.

Peggy shook her head. "I am not sure we ought to trust the nurse. She is alone with them so much of the time."

Louisa-Margaretta had felt some sympathy for the theory that some individual might want to hurt the infants, but at Peggy's tremulous tone, she gave a bark of laughter.

"That woman loves these little things. You cannot be serious."

Peggy made no answer.

"Please, Peggy. Look into my eyes and tell me that Joyce means either child harm."

Peggy did not meet Louisa-Margaretta's gaze. "I saw her."

"Who? Joyce Garvey? Fancy that."

"She was in the woods," Peggy insisted. "When you climbed that tree after William, and I went after you, I saw Joyce meeting a woman there. She let her hold one of the babies!"

"Peggy, we are constantly letting all sorts of women hold these babies. Even Mercy holds them, and don't give me that look. You know anywhere else, it would not be permitted. I myself am holding a baby at this very moment, though I am generally known to dislike them."

Peggy's face looked pained. "Of course I do not think she would harm them. But why meet with strangers in secret? She makes no secret of how strange she finds the Quakers. Could she be looking for families to take them in?"

Louisa-Margaretta had no answer. "Do you think I ought to just waltz in and ask her?"

"No, but you could take Charity over to the superintendents' home and see that both are well."

The little one was beginning to stir. Louisa-Margaretta would have to hurry if she was going to deposit the thing before it started squalling.

"Fine. I will take it, but I'll hurry back."

"Thank you," said Peggy.

"It's supposed to be a cool night."

"You don't have far to go."

That much, at least, was true. Louisa-Margaretta put on her coat to rush across the lawn, but she needn't have bothered. There must have been a small meal at the home of the superintendents, as it seemed everything had already been cleared away. She listened closely for any sound of life on the first floor, but the cook said that both superintendents were in the library.

"I only need to go to the nursery," said Louisa-Margaretta. "Peggy took this little lamb away, and she insisted I return it at this instant. She would have come herself."

Too late, she realised she had not thought of a reason why Peggy had not come over, so she relied on one of her oldest tricks. She stood about with a haughty, detached expression until she got exactly what she wanted.

When she went up and saw Joyce, the old nurse waved her into the room. "Constance won't mind," she said. "Looks as if they're both sleeping, the darlings."

For the first time, Louisa-Margaretta was able to visit the nursery without feeling offended. Constance did look rather angelic in her tiny little cot, and she and Charity were certainly less horrid when they were neither loud nor foul-smelling. Louisa-Margaretta placed Charity in the nurse's arms, surprised at the relief in her limbs when she put her down. Hardly conscious of the movement, she swung her arms.

"Heavy, that one," said Joyce, "but then, they all are."

She adjusted her dress, and Charity began to suckle without opening her eyes.

"You're sure two isn't too many?"

Joyce almost laughed, but something in her tone made Louisa-Margaretta hesitate. "Two, too many, when all I have to do is care for them in this house, with others' food? No, dear. I must say I'm not sure you think to ask many women if nine is too many or twelve."

Louisa-Margaretta glared. "I think that a wife and

mother may be allowed to decide the size of her own family."

The fight went out of Joyce, and she looked sad. "Well, you think wrongly, then, Miss. But never mind that now."

"Good night," Louisa-Margaretta said. "I can see myself out."

But she did not, at least, at first. The strange comment Joyce had made rankled. For the first time in her life, she was in surroundings where she was afforded no particular deference. Her father's money, her mother's family, and her position in society meant nothing. She was only another "friend" who was supposed to be helping. Though at times, it made her conversations much more interesting, especially when she got to argue with Marla about what everyone ought to eat, at other times, she longed for Wycliff Castle. *Oh, to speak a thought aloud without instantly having it contradicted!* Even Judith had become less agreeable than she had once been and more inclined to argue.

Louisa-Margaretta lingered on the stairs, listening to the sounds of the superintendents' life. It was still not late. Any ordinary family would have lit candles and brought out a game of cards. But that family, with its religious bent, would probably be reading the Bible or debating some arcane point of theology. Louisa-Margaretta got enough of that with her mother. She could hardly believe she was so far from Wycliff Castle, yet somehow, she had managed to land in another place ruled by a woman so enamoured of her faith that she could hardly be called God-fearing. Indeed, perhaps God feared the likes of women like Mama and Margaret. If he didn't, he ought to.

"We shall not have another doctor," said the man. It must have been Jacob Lamb, though his voice was more sour than usual. "One disaster, and that's flat. Didn't that man tell us that our people were beyond his expertise and learning?"

"He did learn a great deal while he was here," said Margaret. Her voice was strong, without the bitter note of her husband's. "And consider, it is not only for ailments of the mind that we need a doctor. What if another person should come here from Bethlem with feet that are in a sorry state? We are supposed to be masters of healing."

"And heal, we shall, without another doctor," said Jacob. "I will not have another man like that here again, and as soon as we can decently do so, we must find a foundling home to take the infants."

"That, I shall never consider," said Margaret. "We may as well not even speak of it. They are staying, both of them, for the present. If they were to leave, it would be with a family, not to be sent to some cold place with nobody to care for them."

"We cannot afford it," he said then grumbled, "Joyce's wages will cost us a fortune as it is. Our subscribers do not send us money for this sort of thing. Two children!"

"Hardly a fortune" came the response. "I had to force Joyce to accept the wages she deserves for two. She said she would be paid for one, that a second was no trouble and she didn't like to take money for both. Imagine!"

"Well, I wonder that she required persuasion, then. Perhaps we ought to have let her have it the way she likes it. I daresay she knows children."

"She cares for them and wants what is best for their bodies and their spirits, and that is the first thing. Our first duty is affection!"

"A child's first duty is obedience," said Jacob Lamb sharply.

Louisa-Margaretta stifled a yawn. She was interested in

what the conversation had revealed, but she was not about to stand and listen to Jacob's opinion of what children owed their parents. Though she could ignore most sermons, that sort always tended to prickle at her ears. For when she had been sorely tested, she had decided she owed her parents some sort of obedience. The only thing that had kept her from running through the snow, screaming and tearing at her hair, was a wish to marry against their wishes without completely humiliating them. But if she had found a way to get back to London straightaway, sold all her savings, and thrown herself at Isaac's feet, she still might have had him. She would not be a spinster, working in a very strange position for meagre wages, having thrown in her lot with a man who was probably as mad as anyone at the home.

The thought of Mr Fortescue unsettled her, and she hurried back to whatever comfort the company of the madwomen and their attendants might offer. *Better not to think of him tonight.*

**34**

L ouisa-Margaretta wondered how quickly she could find Judith. After all, the information would be useless to anyone except her friend. She would never have supposed that Jacob Lamb wished to rid the home of both doctors and foundlings.

Instead of hurrying across the lawn again, she took the long way around, though it was colder, and went in the kitchen door. The kitchens had been left completely unattended, even though there was usually at least one person still tidying at that late hour. Since coming to the home, Louisa-Margaretta had become much more familiar with household timetables that would have been foreign to her at Wycliff Castle. She did go to the kitchens occasionally when she was hungry, but she never stopped to think just how dark and unceasing the labor was. Now, since she relied on the goodwill of the not very numerous staff to keep all the ladies in her care happy, she was much better acquainted with those details.

She rushed up the back stairs, thanking her good luck that she did not encounter anyone else. She could go straight upstairs and find Judith, who would be with Mercy.

Only, both of them were gone.

The room had clearly been left in a hurry. Judith always kept it tidy, as if it were a true sickroom. To Louisa-Margaretta, it seemed unnatural to never have so much as a book or a flower out of place. She tried to calm her thoughts. Mercy had not been well, so it was unlikely they had gone far. *But why would they leave the room at all unless she was much improved?*

She went to check on Peggy next. Perhaps she had taken over. But all Louisa-Margaretta could tell was that the luxurious bath her sister-in-law had enjoyed was certainly finished, and there was no sign of her.

It was time to brave the sitting room.

Louisa-Margaretta used to dislike seeing the large group of ladies, but she admitted they had their uses. Though she found gentlemen just as prone to gossip as ladies generally, that group was rather extraordinary. Perhaps it was because they were all prisoners. Though they would be permitted to leave were they to request it, all of them were still trapped by their own minds. Louisa-Margaretta had lived what should have been a life of ease in Wycliff Castle, but she had felt her spirits darken in the wild, inhospitable country. Surely the women were the same. Though life at the home was far from what she was accustomed to, it was far better than any other madhouse. Yet she sensed there was more resentment than piety amongst the people staying there. They wished they could have been left on their own to get on with things, and only the most broken were too far gone to complain.

The sitting room had been abandoned. Unlike the room Judith shared with Mercy, it was quite untidy, though in most circumstances, the ladies would have been reminded to clean it. Work was flung over chairs, plates still had crumbs, and a hearty fire was burning away in the specially constructed grate.

Louisa-Margaretta shivered, trying to remember what the situation had been with the doors. She had gone through the kitchen but only because she had a key to the kitchen door, which she had been sure to lock behind her. *If I had gone through another door, would I have found something unlocked?*

Footsteps sounded in the hall, ones she didn't recognise. They were slow. Louisa-Margaretta would have been less afraid had they been quick, because then she would have been able to follow her instincts and run. Slow footsteps meant whoever was approaching the room was certain of his success. She was all alone, and even if it would have helped to scream, her voice failed her.

Her hands, however, did not completely fail. With a trembling breath, she blew out a candle, and she gripped the candlestick as the hot wax fell on her fingers.

All she had to do, she reflected, was forget the entire philosophy of the home. Their emphasis on each person as a human being, a child of God, must be forgot. If she had been faced with a madman before her Quaker indoctrination, she would have hit him over the head without hesitation. That was all she needed to do, since she had no gun. At least she had her strength and her wits. She could not say why the others had run, but she would be damned if she was going to retreat as well.

Her breathing was steady now. She blew out another candle. Louisa-Margaretta had always been better with her left hand than her right, but she had to arm herself as best as she could. If she were to lose one candlestick, she would have the other. It was a pity there was no time to get to the poker, but keeping it sequestered from many of the women who used the room meant putting it behind fiddly locks. She had no time to free it.

The footsteps slowed, and the door fully opened. Louisa-Margaretta grew still.

"I have weapons," she said, her voice low. "So you'll turn around and leave if you know what's good for you."

No response came at first. Then Louisa-Margaretta heard a strange sound she could not identify. She had blown out two of the brightest candles and had to rely on the light of the fire to see the person shadowed by the door.

"I will not hesitate to hurt you," she said. "Leave, or come in and be damned."

After a sharp intake of breath came a voice that shocked Louisa-Margaretta.

## 35

"Louisa-Margaretta, what on earth?"

Judith squinted into the darkness. Her sight had never been as good as her friend's, but she thought Louisa-Margaretta was brandishing a pair of candlesticks, her eyes glistening with hatred.

The candlesticks lowered. "Judith? Have you seen him, then?"

"Him?"

"Whoever drove everyone out of this wing. Billy, I suppose it must have been, though I would never have thought him violent."

Judith was breathing rapidly. "No, nor I. Nobody was driving people out of the wing. We went to see the baby."

Louisa-Margaretta shook her head, not lowering the candlesticks. "But I was with both of the babies."

Judith stepped into the room, clutching her bundle tightly and hoping her friend would put the candlesticks back soon.

"Yes. But this one is a third."

Though Louisa-Margaretta did not return the candlesticks, she did make her way over, peering at the baby's head. The little one had woken briefly when surrounded by all the women who lived in the wing, but she had gone back to sleep without much fuss.

"I know little of babies," said Louisa-Margaretta, "but having seen the others, I think this one looks rather fat."

Judith loosened her grip on the little one, and Louisa-Margaretta put the candlesticks down on a table.

"She is rather fat." Judith made her way slowly to a chair and sat on the very edge as deliberately as she could. "Peggy has gone to relieve Joyce Garvey, but I am not terribly worried about this one. She's had plenty of milk, clearly, and she looks older."

Louisa-Margaretta took another chair. "Why a third foundling? Can there be so many poor children in this village?"

Judith blinked, looking at the fine eyelashes of the sleeping baby. "Many children are poor, but there are more foundlings here than I would have expected. Perhaps people cannot afford to make a trip to the city. It is not as if there is another haven for them nearby."

"Were I a mother, I am not sure that the scene of a vicious murder would be my first choice."

"They haven't many choices. Quite apart from that, many believe the doctor's death was due to happenstance, not violence."

Still, she clutched the infant a bit tighter. The sense of unease that had forced her to nudge Louisa-Margaretta out the door earlier, to check on the two infants in Joyce's care, was returning. She did not sense that the nurse herself was to blame, as she had been far away when the doctor lost his life. But it seemed likely that someone at the home had killed the poor man, and her suspicions were so wild that she could not share them even with her friend.

"Did anyone give you trouble on your errand?" she asked. "And how did you find the other children? Did you not meet Peggy on your way across the lawn or see any of us by the door? Even Marla was cooing over this one. I could scarcely believe it."

"No. You left them by the door, then?"

"Yes, I convinced them to let me give the poor mite some peace and quiet while we wait for the nurse. But tomorrow, they've all been promised a chance to hold her."

With that, both of them heard commotion in the passageways, the sound of all the ladies making their slow return. Judith hoped Joyce would come with them and take the baby away directly. Though she felt guilty asking her to take on the care of all three, Peggy had insisted upon paying. Though she had murmured something about Percival that made Judith rather wonder whether he would spare any of the money. Peggy, who had married without anything settled on her, had no funds of her own. Percival, who held the purse strings, had not been to visit his wife lately. Perhaps his resolution to leave his dissolute ways and save his marriage was waning in the face of what he had witnessed at the home.

"Judith," said Louisa-Margaretta. "When I went over to see the infants, I wondered about something. Just for a moment, don't let your mind go racing off to strange conclusions when I tell you."

Judith nearly sighed. If what her friend said confirmed her unease, as least she would feel that her conclusions had not been stupid.

"Yes?"

The women had finally arrived.

"Oh, the darling!" one said. "And she looks so well! An elder for the nursery."

Judith and the infant were surrounded, and by the time she handed the child over to Joyce, she and Louisa-Margaretta were deep in the many-headed chore of getting all the ladies off to bed.

## 36

Louisa-Margaretta meant to find her friend first thing in the morning. But Judith and Mercy were already finished with their breakfast by the time she finished attending to the other ladies, and Peggy in particular was not in good spirits. With all the ladies gathered in one room, there would be no chance of speaking privately.

"Might we not all go for a walk?" she asked, knowing almost as soon as she said it that her attempt would be met with failure.

Esther shook her head gravely. "We were promised a visit from the little one," she said. "From Comfort."

Louisa-Margaretta laughed. "Comfort, Constance, and Charity. They make a strange little trio indeed. Like milk-fed furies."

"They are good-enough names," snapped Timofea. "I would hate for my child to be named something silly, like Rose or Jenny. A name ought to have real meaning. They are not going to be babies forever."

"Well, they are babies now," said Marla. "And they will

do little but sleep. Even so, I'm sure Comfort is much more interesting than digging in that infernal garden. It ought to be a mess of mud today anyway."

"Has it been raining?" asked Louisa-Margaretta.

Judith smiled. "You would sleep through anything, wouldn't you? There have been terrible storms since we went to bed."

Louisa-Margaretta sniffed. "Well, there doesn't seem to be anything now."

"Yes, but the place is a mess of mud," said Lucy. "We shouldn't go out of doors until there has been some sun on things."

"If we are to see her, someone has to go," said Louisa-Margaretta. "Judith, will you and Mercy not accompany me?"

"Thou," chorused several of the ladies.

Louisa-Margaretta ignored them. "As I said, Judith, *you* might like the walk, and so might Mercy. And we could look in on this new baby."

"Do look in on her," said Judith, but she was giving Mercy a worried look, as she was rocking and murmuring to herself. "Mercy and I cannot come quite yet, but oh, it would be wonderful for someone to see to the child."

"Yes, see to her," said Lucy. "And bring us back a full report."

Lucy's voice was sincere, but Louisa-Margaretta only glared.

"Why should I go? Walk in all this mud without a horse? Someone will have to shine my boots until they glisten on my return, and I do not intend to do it."

"That's a shock there," said Marla. "And here I was, sure that your ladyship would clean your own boots."

"Fancy the mud, then?" snapped Louisa-Margaretta.

Everyone laughed.

"You're all right," said Marla, leaning back.

"Fine. I do not care who cleans my boots or who brings me a hot cup of tea, but I shall expect both if I am to make this journey twice."

---

## 37

Judith was certain that Louisa-Margaretta had intended to speak with her. Something in her manner suggested it, although they had not been able to find a single moment to speak since the day before.

Though she hated mud, when Louisa-Margaretta went over to fetch the baby, Judith knew she had to seize her chance. If she were to go to the superintendents' home, she could contrive a private conversation with her friend on the way. If she waited, they might not speak for days.

"Come, Mercy," she said politely. "We could use a walk."

Judith had never had a great tolerance for ladies who insisted on always being out of doors. Louisa-Margaretta loved riding and hunting, but even she would accept the occasional afternoon of cards if the Derbyshire weather was particularly foul. But Mercy needed the sun and wind on her face more than anyone Judith had ever met. Fresh air and Bach were the only two things that had any hope of calming her, and a little of either went a long way toward preventing the outbursts that had made her well-known in the home and the village.

Mercy dutifully followed Judith out the door, her face fixed in the way it was when she was about to be out of spirits. Judith hoped their walk would do something. By the time they went outside, Louisa-Margaretta had almost reached the superintendents' home, and Judith thought she might as well wait outside the place with Mercy. Louisa-Margaretta went in the front door, and Judith settled in to watch the sunshine transform the place. In the morning, the home was not an unattractive location. Strange, perhaps, given the size of the buildings, but it was full of the leafy renewal of springtime.

Louisa-Margaretta returned moments later, holding one of the babies in her arms.

"Judith, what the devil are you doing here?"

"Louisa-Margaretta." Judith gave a pointed glance at Mercy.

Louisa-Margaretta gave Mercy one of her usual grins. "Mercy, don't mind me. I will say 'you' and 'devil' and all sorts of words the Quakers don't favor but only when I'm with friends."

Mercy was looking at the door to the superintendents' home.

"We don't need to go in, Mercy," said Judith gently.

"You'd better come," Louisa-Margaretta interjected. "Joyce is not happy this morning, and unless somebody helps her, the home might need to find a new nurse. Hardly ideal when the nursery has multiplied so rapidly."

Judith and Mercy went inside. It felt rude to go directly to the nursery, but nobody came to greet them. The superintendents only employed a small staff and typically liked to greet guests themselves. It had always seemed like a rather comfortable arrangement to Judith, though she knew Louisa-Margaretta despised it.

"Well, you've brought more ladies. I can manage, I'm sure, but it's not like all of them to just lie in bed like this. Especially her."

Joyce was nursing two of the babies at once, one at either side of her on a sofa, each little head in one of her large hands.

"Her?" asked Judith.

"You know, Missus Lamb."

"I cannot imagine her ever sleeping while the sun shines, and it is late already," mused Louisa-Margaretta.

"Miss Bathsheba neither. She comes in quite early," said Joyce stoutly.

Judith frowned. That seemed an exaggeration. She rarely saw Bathsheba do any sort of work early in the morning and had often heard her complain about how being compelled to come down and have breakfast was itself akin to punishment.

"I'll look in on them," she said. "Perhaps you ladies could remain here?"

Both Joyce and Louisa-Margaretta nodded to show they understood. They were to watch Mercy, who did not yet seem out of spirits but might at any moment have a fit.

"Very well."

She was glad to leave the crowded nursery, but as she approached the private rooms of the Lamb family, she felt unsettled. Surely the duty ought to fall to someone else.

## 38

The Lamb family lived plainly, as much by necessity as by the virtue of their religion. The building where they lived, though it might have been spacious for their family, was filled with guests of the home. With the addition of a room full of infants under Joyce's care, it felt more like a boarding house than a home with every luxury. Judith wondered what its previous owners would have made of the place as it had become.

The Lambs had a small sitting room that was private for the family, with two bedrooms just off it. In the sitting room was where Judith found Margaret. She was seated on the floor, her head bent over her clasped hands, praying fervently.

"Grieved rather than angry."

Judith, clergyman's daughter to the last, instinctively turned away. She was not going to interrupt a lady at prayer, no matter Joyce's complaints. But she turned back, seeing that Margaret had not even noticed her presence. She looked older than Judith had ever seen, her skin pale and glistening with sweat as she murmured to herself.

"Margaret," Judith said, "I'm so sorry. May I speak with thee?" The Quaker forms of address flew out of her mouth, and she felt less awkward using them than she might have. The woman stared at her then rose with some difficulty.

"My husband," she said. "He is just there. He is dead."

Judith realised how seldom she saw Margaret simply stand still. The woman was so active that certain irreverent residents of the home liked to joke that she neither ate nor slept. But there she stood, staring past the doorway.

In the other room, the bedroom, was a figure on the bed. Drawing closer, Judith recognised the superintendent. She had helped lay the dead to rest her whole life and was less alarmed by the sight of him than she was by the behavior of his wife.

Judith walked over to the dead man, tucked the blanket about him, and said a prayer. Then she went back to Margaret.

"Poison," Margaret whispered.

"Shall I go for the magistrate?" asked Judith. "Or I could send someone? Sit, please." Judith was also used to dealing with the bereaved, but she was unprepared to treat Margaret with the gentle and cautious manner she usually reserved for those in the throes of madness.

But the word "magistrate" seemed to change something in the woman.

"No. I am so sorry, Judith. My husband had a fit while he was sleeping. And he died."

For the first time, she looked directly at Judith. "Perhaps you can help me notify everyone at the home. We have a great deal of work ahead."

And before Judith could take another look at the private rooms of the Lamb family or enquire what Margaret had meant when she whispered, "Poison," she found herself gently guided back into the passageway.

## 39

The residents and staff of the home were apparently destined to be importuned by every subscriber on earth. Visitors poured in, sitting with Margaret for hours and getting underfoot in the kitchen. The first day, there were many, and the second day, there were more. Louisa-Margaretta and Judith had no chance to visit the superintendents' home after their troubling encounter there, but they saw the carriages arriving and noticed the men and women streaming up to the door of the place.

"I suppose it may help," said Judith. "One of them may be able to assist us in learning more about the killer."

"You suppose wrongly, Judith," said Louisa-Margaretta. "They will keep us all here, bound by their tedious presence, and not help one whit. How are we to find a murderer in such a crowd?"

The two of them were out for a walk with all the women, Mercy a bit subdued but quite ready to escape to the quiet of the trees. Peggy always wished to visit the babies, but since all of them were with Joyce, that would mean braving the visitors. Judith and Louisa-Margaretta, in the chaos following the superintendent's death, had not been able find one moment to converse unobserved. Judith wondered what her friend had been on the verge of telling her and whether it still mattered now that Jacob was dead.

Peggy, meanwhile, still thought only of the babies' welfare.

"I'm not sure she can feed them all," Peggy had confessed to Judith. "Three children? I have heard of mothers feeding two and wet nurses feeding a great deal more, but I wonder if they will all grow as they ought."

"As a nurse, she should know, I suppose," said Judith, trying not to let her own doubts show.

Joyce was all confidence, but it did seem rather unnatural to her. Many of the stories she heard about twins included one or both being sickly or the mother dying or other horrors, and three did seem rather unreasonable.

"Would you go see them, Louisa-Margaretta?" asked Peggy. "I know Joyce Garvey has tired of me, but you don't mind bothering her."

"Yes, I don't care how much she hates the sight of me, but neither do I wish to go."

"Just for a moment. We will be sitting down to eat our picnic soon, and Judith and I will both stay."

Judith saw how drawn Peggy's face was. She had truly taken to the third foundling, who had come in the night and forced the hearts of the company open even wider. And she was much more interested in the children than she was in her duty to the women, though nobody could fault the devotion with which she continued to perform it.

"Perhaps you could learn something from one of the visitors," Judith said to Louisa-Margaretta. "They are all of one community, after all. One of them might know something about one of these poor souls that we would not know."

"That *you* would not know after all these months here?" Louisa-Margaretta looked over at the house then gave an exasperated sigh. "Fine. It is rather dull here. But I am not going to spend the afternoon with a herd of mewling infants. One glance, Peggy, then I shall return."

Clarinda heard and laughed. Peggy only smiled, seeming grateful that her sister-in-law was going, however reluctantly.

The ladies returned to have their lunch, and Judith tried to eat well. She would need her strength. With both Margaret and Bathsheba seeing their visitors and laying a member of their family to rest, all the women working at the home were needed every hour of the day. The ladies and gentlemen who were visiting, offering to help, were not quite willing to take on the duties that would have been the most helpful.

As Judith was serving some cold meat to Mercy, watching to make sure all the ladies got their fill, Louisa-Margaretta returned with a satisfactory report. "The new one is sleeping, and so are the two others. According to Joyce, this is what one must expect from a baby, particularly a baby who happens to be well-fed. Might I have your permission?"

She murmured something that should have been a prayer but might well have been a curse and reached for one of the baskets of food.

"Judith," she said, "they want to speak with you also. Go to the drawing room. Only, make haste, or I shall perish of boredom here."

"Boring you, are we?" growled Marla.

"Yes, my darling. If anyone knows any scandalous plays

or passages from forbidden novels, this would be the time to remember them."

The ladies roared with laughter, and Louisa-Margaretta grinned as she sat down to get started on her food.

Judith sat very near her so she could whisper. "What have you learned? Who has come to see the family?"

"You must go and see for yourself, Judith. I shan't be revealing any secrets."

**40**

———

When Judith went into the drawing room of the superintendents' home, a man was there, and she apologised. She'd nearly left the room, too, until she saw him.

He had clearly not slept well, and he bore all the signs of one who had traveled a great distance without being able to shave or change. Yet his face, his figure, and his bearing were all even more handsome than she remembered, and she found herself nearly trembling as she turned away from the door, her hand still on the knob.

He did not greet her.

She found her words first. "Mr Ramsbury. Good afternoon."

She wasn't supposed to say that. It was not a greeting allowed in the circle, and usually, after so many months, she would have remembered. But her mind was entirely occupied with remembering other things.

He raised a hand then lowered it. "Miss St Clair," he said. "I hope I find thee well. Find *you* well, that is."

Judith was not the only one confused about language.

Even the act of addressing each other, which had once been ever so natural, was strange and bewildering.

They should not have been in a room together unchaperoned. But neither mentioned it. Judith wondered why the drawing room was not full of visitors then recalled that they were most likely in the parlor with the ladies of the family.

"Please, won't you sit," he said hastily, and she found a chair, which she hoped would help keep any trembling from his view.

Judith thought she could hardly speak, yet her time at the home had prepared her. She was able to force air through her lungs and speech through her mouth, even in spite of her feelings. It could hardly be more difficult than speaking in a soothing voice to Mercy when the poor woman was screaming.

"I hope you are well," she said. "I understand I am to congratulate you on your marriage."

The bald statement was nearly too much for her, and she gripped the arm of her chair. But once it was said, she told herself she need not ever say it again. The acute part of the pain would be short, at least.

"M-Marriage? Where did you hear of such a thing?"

She gave a wan smile. "Everyone here speaks highly of you, especially the Lambs."

"I am not well-known to the Lambs."

To her, it was an accusation of falsehood and made her cold to hear it. "I did not say such a thing, only that they frequently speak of thee."

But she wondered if she was telling the truth. Certainly, whenever she heard the name Morgan on the lips of any of his Quaker friends, she was thrown into a whirlwind of emotion, and it was all she could do to try to concentrate on whatever was before her to disguise the sensibility. She was conscious, often, of failure, particularly with their guests. All of them had plenty of practice in concealment, a necessary evil when one had struggled with madness. Judith had often noticed that where she might just manage to keep something from Bathsheba or Lucy, a young woman such as Marla would find her out and even try to comfort her.

"I wonder that they do," he said quietly. "I used to be more of a presence here. Before."

She heard an accusation in that too. But she had not forced him to stay away.

"Peggy has benefitted from her time here," she said. "As have I, truth be told. But thou art always welcome."

He must have heard the cold formality in her voice. Though "thou" was supposed to be more familiar, when Judith used it, she meant to distance herself from the pain of intimacy.

And Morgan responded in kind. "That is also what I have heard. Though, not from you, Judith, because you never responded to any of my letters."

He had written to her a great deal, and she had read each letter with a mixture of pleasure and pain, until they had stopped coming altogether. Of course, it would not have been proper for him to write to her directly, so the letters were to her whole family. But her father, though he was not sophisticated, must have thought it right to send them on to her. Either that, or Miriam was responsible for forwarding them.

She thought that was more likely, and it gave her a pang. She had never reconciled with her sister after she left, and the only lines she did get from Miriam were simple and cold, as if their aunt Leah were sitting beside her and forcing her to write. But Miriam must have understood that Judith would want to read every one of Morgan's letters.

Miriam would understand why Judith wanted to keep them too. She had kept every one and still treasured them. When she was feeling low, if Mercy was fast asleep, she often lit a candle to read them all over again.

But she was not going to tell him that.

"I can tell thee anything thou mayst wish to know at this very moment," she said. "Only ask me."

His face, which had been rigid, suddenly had a hint of a smile.

"Well, then. Who is responsible for these terrible murders?"

She was silent but only for a moment. "I would say if I knew. I would tell the magistrate."

"But if you only had a suspicion?"

When she made no answer, he continued, "I am quite sure you and Miss Haddington have some notions. In fact, I find the matter of her coming here after the first death rather interesting."

"Most consider the doctor's death to be no more than a tragic incidence of misfortune, not misadventure."

"But the two of you have other ideas." His face grew serious. "Please, you must tell me. If there is anything I can do to put a stop to this, I will take your word. Only tell me."

Judith longed to confide in him but knew it to be too dangerous. "I wish I knew."

"Once, you would have shared even your suspicions, Miss St Clair."

The title wounded her. She heard the change in his voice, but she was not going to give in.

"I will not share anything that might harm an innocent person. When there is news, you will hear it."

"That is all, then? I might learn of a murderer just when everyone else does? And I might hope before this entire place collapses and the inhabitants are sent to Bethlem or somewhere just as horrid?"

Her face was set. She would not cry in front of him. "I have done more to keep our guests here from being sent to a place like that than you can ever claim."

He started. "Miss St Clair."

"I have fed the sick and cleaned up after those who could not find their chamber pot, and listened to screamed oaths in the night that most men would have trouble imagining. And all for no thanks from the likes of the men who were running the place, may God bless them."

"I know everyone is very thankful. I am very thankful myself, and—"

"You have chosen to come without a care for my feelings, accusing me of all sorts of things. Using what was once a friendship to try to pry at my thoughts."

Her anger was growing slowly but insistently. *How could an engaged man come see me alone, looking for information he has no right to?*

"Judith," he said more insistently, "I pray you would still consider me a friend."

"Then trust me," she said more loudly than she had meant to, whipping her head so that she faced him directly. "I would not let anyone come to harm here. But in return, there is an area where you must use your influence."

She had forgotten to call him "thou" in her anger. He looked wrong-footed still and only nodded at first. "I will, if you only ask it of me."

"Make sure no harm comes to the children. It was after the first foundling arrived that the doctor was murdered, and it would be silly to pretend there is no connection."

He started. "But... they are all just infants, are they not? And their families did not want them?"

His words were a rather melancholy reminder to her of the great differences between their families and their upbringings. Mr Morgan Ramsbury had known troubles, of course, but for him to think foundlings unwanted spoke of such ignorance of most of the populace that it made Judith's head ache.

"Their families love them," she said firmly. "And if they were able to feed and support another child, I am quite sure they would. The leaving was an act of the purest love."

He still looked doubtful. "I am sure we cannot make assumptions about every single family, especially when they do not tend to stay to answer questions."

"We cannot assume that they would keep a child if they felt they had any alternative?"

He would not give way. "None of the families of these foundlings stayed to make such claims."

Judith paused. "Well."

"One of them did, then? To explain a choice others would not have made?"

"Is it so difficult to imagine such a choice when they see the situation here?" she asked gently. "Of course, nobody is overly concerned with ostentatious wealth, and there is plain dress, but we always have a great deal of food."

"Perhaps not," he said, yielding to her arguments, as he often did. Because Mr Morgan Ramsbury had respected her mind and listened to her, as no other man had, when she was with him, Judith had always felt a sense of power—and giddiness, yes, because a single glance at him was enough to put roses in her cheeks, but she also felt her own influence. She had wondered whether that was because of his being a member of the Society of Friends. At least, after she found out and broke things off, she had wondered if his courtesy was universal among the Quakers.

But her more recent experiences had proved that untrue. While many of the men at the home did respect her, it was more common that they ignored her. And more than one showed blatant contempt for her opinions the way the doctor had.

In fact, the superintendent had been similarly dismissive. And now both were dead.

She thought there might be meaning in that. And she thought of all the women at the home, ones she'd thought she knew well. It was a place like no other, where people who had once been complete strangers knew that she talked in her sleep and could probably recognise all of her stockings and hats, not just her modest collection of dresses. They not only took meals together but also whiled away rainy days and talked through the worst of nights.

But she could not hold the thought because she found Mr Morgan Ramsbury still looking at her.

"I fancy summer is not like this at all up north," he said. "At least, based on how cold the spring was."

Judith remembered how their days were together and knew he was remembering as well—their favorite tree and the way they'd braved the mud and wind in order to steal hours together away from her family or his.

"I suppose you will not be there often," she said, her voice breaking. She tried to recover. It was humiliating for her to learn of his marriage from others. He had not even written a line. "You might have told me," she said, her voice stronger now.

"Told you?" he asked. "I do not understand."

"No," she said. "I suppose you do not. You must excuse me."

**41**

———

Louisa-Margaretta could not get any more distant than the garden, though she would have loved to spend the afternoon away from the home. Since they were short of people who might have helped with the ladies, she had decided they should bring the lot of them out to work in the afternoon sun, assuming Judith would approve. Only days ago, Margaret had been going on about how May was the best time to distill herbs and how they all were going to work on that task together. But Margaret and Bathsheba had abandoned them to their labours. And Louisa-Margaretta was beginning to feel that was rather unfair. Yes, they had lost a member of their family, but at least they were not mad. Surely they could begin to see to the ladies again, allowing some well-deserved rest for those who had stepped into the breech.

"Don't pull up the purslane again!" cried Marla, glaring at Louisa-Margaretta from under her bonnet. "Our stews will suffer if you thin out the whole garden."

"I thought it was a weed," snapped Louisa-Margaretta.

"And I've never liked it. I'm sure our stews will be better thanks to my work."

"It does grow like a weed," said Clarinda, who had already gotten through half of her row of cabbages. She was so tidy about her weeding, and she moved silently. Louisa-Margaretta was surprised to hear her say anything.

"It does," said Deborah, and the women exchanged smiles.

Louisa-Margaretta ought to have been happy that Clarinda was beginning to speak and make friends, but she was out of temper. "In a few minutes, Judith will come to rescue me from this garden, and you can all thank her." She stood. Though she was tempted to ask the other ladies how they did such work without their backs hurting, the first time she had asked, she received only laughter as an answer. She hunted all day without complaining of soreness or fatigue, yet a mere half hour in the kitchen garden left her longing for relief.

Walking over to the wall, she saw what seemed to be a ripe gooseberry warmed by the sun. She would rather have had a hearty piece of ham, but until dinner, food would not appear before them. Though the home was rather brilliant in its acknowledgment that people who were mad needed to eat well and keep up their strength, that did not stretch to allowing anyone to raid the kitchens between meals. Louisa-Margaretta, who had grown up sneaking just as many treats as she liked from indulgent cooks and kitchen maids, found that rather trying.

Timofea was the only one who saw the face Louisa-Margaretta made as the sour berry accosted her tongue. She giggled, and Louisa-Margaretta composed her features.

"Timofea, you've missed some of the weeds there.

Unless they are weeds we are meant to eat, the way we choke down purslane."

"I've always rather fancied purslane," said someone behind her. "At least when the wine is of a good quality."

"Percival," said Louisa-Margaretta, her eyes narrowing. "You're not supposed to be in this section."

"Might I have a word? Is Peggy here?"

"No, and you can't have a word."

But she had forgotten that Betsey was with the group, her basket brimming with cucumbers, artichokes, nasturtium flowers, and all sorts of vegetables.

"Go," said Betsey. "I'll be here until you've finished talking to your brother."

Louisa-Margaretta nodded and walked to the garden's entrance. Percival was leaning on the wall like the decorative gentleman he was. She, who had never worked a day in her life before the home, had suddenly begun to find men without professions rather irritating. *If only Percival would go back to the army!* Then he wouldn't have time to moon about, troubling her about Peggy.

"Will Peggy be out, do you think?" he asked as if intending to irritate her.

"Someone had to stay with the ladies who wished for the peace of the parlour. I should have done it myself."

"So she is not coming."

"How should I know? I'm not going to be the peacemaker between you and your wife. You should go see Mama. She would love such an errand."

"Come with me. Come back to Wycliff Castle and see her."

"No, she would not wish me to come back, not without a husband."

"She would always wish to be near you. Don't you understand? She is our mother, and she loves all of us."

For a moment, Louisa-Margaretta was sorely tempted. Try as she might, she could not contradict Percival. For all her arguments with her parents, the bitter shock of their move to Wycliff Castle, and the fumbled attempts at matchmaking that had followed, she felt the love without needing to think of it. If she were to return after her sojourn in London and at the home, perhaps there might be at least some weeks in which matrimonial concerns would not trump the comforts of home. She need never touch the kitchen garden, and she could hunt to her heart's content.

Then she remembered her promise to Mr Fortescue.

"I cannot simply leave," she snapped. "I have work to do here."

She knew he would think she meant weeding the garden, looking after the ladies, and helping keep the home from collapsing under the dual burdens of the foundlings and the murdered men.

*Let him think that,* she decided. If he knew the truth, he would be horrified.

And if she wanted to have any hope of keeping the truth from her family, she needed to discover it right away. She looked into the distance, squinting, hoping for any sign of Judith.

## 42

———

Judith's spirit felt as if it had vanished from her body. She wandered back to her rooms, expecting to find Mercy, before remembering that she was with the larger group of ladies. They were probably confined to the sitting room. Even at the home, certainly the only institution of its kind that recognised the spirit and suffering of its inhabitants, there was a general feeling that subscribers ought not to see *all* of the ladies, only those who were well or very nearly well and had been invited to dine with the superintendent.

He was superintendent no longer, Judith realised. The man who had seen his role as a calling from God, even if Judith did not think he was perfectly fit to perform it, would never fulfill any part of his duties ever again. His poor wife and daughter would be run off their feet, trying to see to everyone's needs as they were grieving. For the first time, Judith's thoughts flitted away from Mr Ramsbury as she remembered how difficult it had been when her mother died. She had not been prostrate with grief, as she had to care for Miriam, her brothers, and even her father. Later, she learned that the most important reason behind her aunt Leah's decision to stay with the family was Judith's lack of appetite. In trying to nurse others through the worst of it, she had grown weak and gaunt. She ought to be making sure the same did not happen to the superintendent's family, atoning for her judgement of the man and the unkind words she had used with him.

But she could not bring herself to go near their residence. Instead, she found Mercy in the parlour and gave tight-lipped smiles to Peggy and the rest of the group as she gently shepherded her charge away. Louisa-Margaretta was arguing with Marla over whether they ought to ask the kitchen for beef with their dinner and did not see Judith's face or notice that she was quiet.

Once she was with only Mercy, Judith began to speak. She stopped hiding all of her feelings, though she did think it would be better not to cry if she could possibly help it. Her voice was strained and raspy, but Mercy did not seem to notice.

"Let's go outside, then, Mercy." Judith thought she had done rather well spending many months without addressing the woman as if she were a child. Yet taking on a governess's strict tone was the only way she could manage the feelings that seemed shot into her body like so many thorns. She understood the metaphor of Cupid's arrow at last. A dozen arrows had gone into her, their tips dark and painful, and only by getting as far away from the home as possible could she begin to pull them out.

"Come on, then. A walk will do us good." Judith hated the tone of the words, but her body was drawn to the outdoors. She felt like a wounded animal. *Is this the pull*

*Louisa-Margaretta feels all the time?* If so, it was hardly a wonder that her friend ran off so often to ride horses and scramble after game.

The walk helped her as soon as it began, but she still felt as if she must run. Yet she was near collapse even with the walking. *Oh, how will my poor heart ever heal?* She would never have believed Mr Morgan Ramsbury's familiarity or his surprise that she should even care to be included in the news of his marriage. Sure, she had heard enough warnings of men who loved and discarded young ladies, but like most, she had thought herself immune to such creatures. That was Louisa-Margaretta's weakness, not hers. She had misjudged him, true, but she had also misjudged herself.

Judith walked quickly, panting, without stopping. She came to a clearing in the woods where she finally stood for a moment, trying to listen.

"God is always speaking to us," her father often told his children, and once, after her mother's death, Judith had been unhappy enough to admit she did not hear His voice.

"I hear only birdsong," she had said to Papa, hoping he would contradict her.

"That is His voice, Judith," he had responded. "The song of the birds, the light through the branches, the rushing of the stream."

Judith started. She could hear the stream but also a splash.

Mercy was sitting in the stream, picking up cold stones and throwing them back into the water. She did not laugh, but she gave a childish smile. It was an amusing activity, it seemed, even for a woman who had not spoken in years.

"Mercy!" cried Judith, coming back to herself. The dismay she had felt at being crossed in love quickly gave way to panic. "You'll catch your death! You must come out, Mercy, please."

Hers was no longer the voice of a stern governess but that of a pleading child. She had not been paying attention, and Mercy had already started to shiver. As Judith helped her charge out of the stream, she felt certain that her inattentiveness would not go unpunished.

**43**

———

Louisa-Margaretta tried to speak to Judith all evening, but she could not get her friend to leave Mercy's side for a moment.

The fire must be perfect. Mercy was sweating, covered in so many blankets that she probably would have perished from thirst if Judith had not been at her side with broth.

"Judith, I still haven't the foggiest notion when the murderer will strike again. Yes, our dear Mercy has a cold, but I need your mind to be turned to other things."

With a trembling voice, Judith said, "Mercy ought not to have suffered. Mercy, I neglected you."

"Poppycock," said Louisa-Margaretta tartly. She noticed that Mercy's eyes were closed. "Mercy, I'm sure you will soon be well. Judith, Bathsheba has been hiding something about her father. I'm sure of it."

"Oh, merciful heavens!" Judith turned to her.

Louisa-Margaretta tried and failed to hide her smile of triumph. Judith would be forced to join her in her inquiries.

"Bathsheba does not like speaking with all the mourners," said Judith carefully. "We cannot fault her for that."

"So you have noticed her behavior is strange. I knew it, Judith!"

"Please." Judith turned back to Mercy, who was stirring. "Louisa-Margaretta, I cannot help you. I must stay at Mercy's bedside until she is well."

*That may be some time,* thought Louisa-Margaretta, but she did not say so. Even the most coldhearted of ladies would have been able to see easily that Judith was suffering with enough guilt to last much longer than the duration of Mercy's illness.

So she went alone to find Bathsheba. Since some of the ladies had retired early, Peggy agreed to see to the rest. Louisa-Margaretta almost floated across the quiet grounds. Only since she had begun to bear the burden of caregiving was she able to feel the glorious liberation that came from caring only for herself.

With polite murmurs, she managed to get around the ladies who were still sitting with Margaret and up to the second floor of the superintendents' home. The doors to their rooms were all ajar, but she found nobody there. The nursery's door was closed, but in response to her knock came the scrape of a chair.

"I will be with you in one moment." But it was several moments before the door opened. "What is it?" asked Bathsheba.

Louisa-Margaretta pushed past her, as it seemed she would not be invited in. "Bathsheba," she said, trying to make her voice warm. "Where has Joyce gone with the babies?"

"They went to take some air, I believe." Bathsheba sat in a chair. Her eyes looked tired, and her arms were crossed firmly across her chest.

Judith would have thought of a clever, subtle approach.

But Louisa-Margaretta did not have any patience for the sort of chat neither of them would enjoy and decided she must be direct. "Well, before they return. I wanted to ask you about your father."

Bathsheba nearly jumped. "Keep your voice down! You'll wake her!"

Louisa-Margaretta had assumed Joyce had taken them all, but one of the little ones with fair skin and moist lips was fast asleep in her crib, not stirring in the least in spite of Bathsheba's objections.

"You can tell me what you wish about your father," she continued, not bothering to keep your voice down. "It is all quite safe with me. I promised Mr Fortescue that I would look into the death of his brother, and whoever killed your father must have done it, don't you think?"

To her surprise, Bathsheba did not deny that murder had been done in both cases. But she tossed her head. "Mr Fortescue cared nothing for his brother. I can't imagine it means anything to him."

Louisa-Margaretta did not answer right away, and Bathsheba nodded.

"If he has not told thee anything about what passed between him and his brother, he is worse than I thought. I would never trust that man."

As it happened, Louisa-Margaretta was quite sure that Mr Fortescue *was* untrustworthy. But she noticed that Bathsheba had not answered her question.

"This place is crawling with people of your community," she said. "Would they not wish to know that there is a murderer here, someone who killed your father?"

At that, Bathsheba stood, her arms falling to her sides as she glared at Louisa-Margaretta. "Thou mayst leave. Yes, the place is crawling with Quakers. That's because the home was created for Quakers, and we ought not to have welcomed others here who do not understand our ways. I will tell my mother where thou hast gone."

"Would you send Joyce away, then? Simply because she does not share your faith?"

A strange expression spread over Bathsheba's features. "Perhaps. We do not need her."

Louisa-Margaretta glanced up at the ceiling, her shoulders collapsing in a sigh. Because Bathsheba had been good enough to watch one sleeping baby for less than an hour, she seemed to fancy herself an expert.

"I don't intend to leave," said Louisa-Margaretta. "And by the way, Judith and I have been performing your duties. This little interlude is the first moment I've had to myself in days, and it's not particularly easy with all these murders leaving the ladies of the home rather more sensible than usual."

Bathsheba looked at the door. "I shall return to my duties soon," she said crisply. "Right away, if thou wilt leave us."

"I will not be leaving. And I remain interested in anything you can tell me about your father. Or even about either of the brothers Fortescue."

Bathsheba looked away. "That is not possible. If thy vanity will keep thee here, well, thou must stay out of my sight."

## 44

"I will be well," said Mercy.

It made Judith think of her mother, always calm, even in a sickbed.

Then she started. *Mercy is speaking!*

"Mercy," she said slowly. "Your fever is very high."

For a moment, Judith wondered if she were hallucinating under the influence of a fever.

But Mercy spoke again. "Where is my husband?"

Judith said nothing, so Mercy continued.

"You can leave, Miss. He will care for me."

Judith froze. Mercy seemed recovered enough to speak, yet she did not know that her husband had died. She tried to think whether Mercy had even been told the information. Judith had tried to take every care not to pretend Mercy was absent, speaking in a hushed voice with Louisa-Margaretta whenever they discussed the murder.

"What is your husband's name?" she asked, scarce believing Mercy knew.

"Ludlow Fortescue," she breathed, her eyes shining. "He is a good man."

Judith found herself ready to disagree, her lip curling. She stammered, "M-Mr Fortescue, you said?" trying to hide her incredulity.

Mercy shook her head violently, which appeared to make her dizzy. "That is his brother. My husband is Mr Ludlow Fortescue."

Judith blinked. "Yes. I have met both your husband and his brother."

Mercy's eyes were filled with tears, but she made no move to wipe them away. "His brother would have ruined me," she said quietly. "Did ruin me. Ludlow would hear of nothing but our marrying, though we were strangers to each other then. He would not let me bring a child into the world without a husband to give the babe a name."

Judith took Mercy's hand. "He sounds like a very good man," she said quietly.

"There was no child in the end. Because I was sick. Ludlow always wanted children."

"And you, Mercy?" asked Judith, her heart lifting. At last, she could ask her charge exactly what she wanted. "Mercy, where do you wish to live, and how do you wish to spend your days?"

"Sleeping," said Mercy with a soft smile. She sank into her pillow, and before Judith could ask her anything else, Mercy's breathing became slow and peaceful.

## 45

Louisa-Margaretta had to send for Mr Fortescue, though she had Margaret do it, of course. Coming from an unmarried woman, the invitation would be most improper. But she only mentioned to Margaret that he was a friend of her brother's and she wished that he might be summoned from the village. He was at the door within the hour, though even the summer sun was beginning to look rather low in the sky, and the household really should have been busy with preparations for their evening repast.

Of course, Louisa-Margaretta should not have been free to see him. With Judith never leaving Mercy's side, Peggy and Louisa-Margaretta were run off their feet, caring for all the other ladies. Louisa-Margaretta was sure she could not be spared if neither of the Lamb ladies came to help. But she was lucky, for one of the visitors, only one, was a useful sort of woman. Her name was Mary Dunn, and she was about the age of Louisa-Margaretta's mother. Mama always wore fine gowns and made herself presentable for even the humblest visit, whereas Mary

Dunn seemed quite enamoured with the doctrine regarding plain dress in Quakers. Her clothing was clean but exceedingly understated, and she had the women set aside their embroidery in order to help her repair those pieces of furniture that were wobbly or stained. "Why wait for men to do it when we can do it ourselves?" she asked. Louisa-Margaretta might have applauded the sentiment had she not been forced to sit on the floor, struggling with an errant chair leg.

Louisa-Margaretta was glad to be called to the superintendents' home when Mary was there to take her place, for it meant she could get away for at least an hour. Mr Fortescue was waiting for Louisa-Margaretta in the sitting room.

For a moment, when she saw him, she forgot his threats and remembered only the swooping sensation that had overcome her when he clutched her form to his, greedy for her affection. She wondered not for the first time whether marrying him would really be so miserable as she had imagined.

"You had something to tell me, my little one?" he asked.

Louisa-Margaretta looked behind her, checking that they had not been overheard. Though she had taken care to leave the door to the room open, nobody was nearby. She hated the way he made her worry about the tongues of others.

"You had something to tell me," she said sternly. "I spoke to someone here who said you were not forthcoming about your brother."

"Who would say such a thing?"

Louisa-Margaretta swallowed. "I've no intention of telling you."

"I might have more information to give you about my

brother's dealings in London. But you would not be so naive as to expect such information to be free, surely?"

"You would not be so naive as to expect a promise of marriage from me. That is, to expect such a promise if I cannot find out what happened to your brother because you have not been honest with me."

"I have never been accused of being honest with anyone," he said firmly. "I am surprised at you, Miss Haddington, I must confess." His expression was one of amusement.

She found herself staring, her admiration for his form mixed with a disbelief at his lack of morals. "You were horrified when he died," she said. "Would you lie to me so I fail, never seeking justice for your brother?"

"Is that what I ought to love best?" he asked, stroking his chin. "Justice? Goodness me."

Louisa-Margaretta frowned. She could find no trace of the man who had been distraught at his brother's death. Mr Fortescue, however shocked he might have been, seemed to have returned to the debonair personality she had encountered in London.

"Name your price, then," she said.

"And you will pay it?" he asked, looking both pleased and surprised.

"No. But I should be curious to know what it was."

He went to the door, beginning to pull it shut, and Louisa-Margaretta's stomach lurched. She ought not to have asked such a question. But the hunger in Mr Fortescue's eyes sparked a twin in Louisa-Margaretta, and it was the only antidote she had ever felt to the pain that had plagued her every day since Isaac abandoned her. She did not know the same pleasure, but the knowledge that she was betraying a man who had once been her beloved was more powerful than the sadness she ought to feel at betraying herself.

"Louisa-Margaretta" came a quiet voice as the door that Mr Fortescue had just shut opened. "Please excuse me, Mr Fortescue," Judith said with a stiff change in her posture that bore some resemblance to a curtsy. "I require a few moments with my friend to discuss one of our ladies."

**46**

―――――

Judith went out to the kitchen garden. She did not look behind her to see if Louisa-Margaretta was following, but she knew exactly how Orpheus must have felt. She scarcely believed her friend was behind her, and it took all the self-discipline and patience she had honed in the home for her to keep from checking.

Of course, Louisa-Margaretta soon spoke, which confirmed she had unwillingly followed her. "He was about to tell me something rather pertinent! Why did you pull me away, Judith? It's as if you have no proper feeling for the people who are falling down dead around us."

Judith almost shuddered. Though Louisa-Margaretta had seen her share of death, she had never lost anyone close and felt that mourning clothes were tedious and funerals were a pointless rite.

But though Louisa-Margaretta was unfeeling, that was all the more reason to suppose her in danger.

"Thee must come with me," said Judith.

She heard voices coming from the window and dropped

to her knees. "Start pulling the weeds out. If we are working, nobody will think to join us."

Louisa-Margaretta, still looking as brash as she had with Mr Fortescue, only laughed. "Why did you say 'thee' to me? Have the Quakers made you one of them?"

She settled on her knees, languidly pulling two weeds then touching her hair.

Judith sighed. "You ought to know better, Louisa-Margaretta. After all my life with my father then many months with the Quakers, I hardly know what I am."

Louisa-Margaretta softened. "Well, should you learn, I'm sure my cousin would be most intrigued to hear."

Judith tried not to cry, which rendered her unable to speak.

Louisa-Margaretta threw the weeds she had plucked aside. They would certainly take root and grow again. She patted Judith's shoulder. "Save your tears. Oh, Judith, you cannot be tiresome and cry at every joke."

Judith frowned, pulling away from her friend's hand. "We should not joke about any of this, Louisa-Margaretta. The situation with Mr Fortescue is most grave."

"Oh, Judith, I do not wish to play his games. But I begin to wonder whether he really would hurt my reputation. Indeed, he seems rather fond of me."

Judith's voice grew strong again. "That cannot be true. Mercy told me that he... that he is not such a man."

Seeing her friend's skepticism, Judith knew she had to be more explicit. She whispered the story to Louisa-Margaretta, warning her that Mr Fortescue could well be the murderer they were seeking. He had deceived them all, and there was certainly no love lost between him and his brother.

But Louisa-Margaretta only sighed. "An elder brother

would never kill the younger. Judith, consider. Why would he? I'm going to go back in and ask him."

"No!" cried Judith, then she lowered her voice. "You should avoid him at every cost."

"What I should do and what I plan to do are very different things," said Louisa-Margaretta, striding back into the house.

**47**

———

When Louisa-Margaretta went over to dinner, she was surprised to find both Margaret and Bathsheba sitting down to dine with the ladies.

"I did not expect you," she said to Bathsheba, who glared at her.

"After such insults, how would it be possible for me to fail to come? Thy opinion of me must be low indeed."

Her voice was not particularly low, although it was a sacred rule of the home that no squabbling should take place in front of those who needed caretaking. Marla laughed, and even Betsey, who was quietly setting out a cabbage dish, permitted herself a small smile.

"I'm sure I don't know what you mean," said Louisa-Margaretta. "But I appreciate the feelings of honor that compelled you across the lawn."

"Louisa-Margaretta," said Margaret, her voice sharp and tired. "Come sit. Have something to eat. Our dinner today is quite full. The kitchen garden has been thriving under thy supervision."

"Under *our* supervision, I thank thee," said Marla.

"I must speak with my sister-in-law, I am afraid. Could one of you show me to her?"

All at once, she felt she could not take one more moment of Marla's jokes or Bathsheba's sulks. She had to solve the murder, the thought of which had wearied her for days, and only Peggy would understand that she needed information from Mr Fortescue to do so. Peggy was apparently out for a walk, and Louisa-Margaretta was more than glad of the excuse to stalk through woods she knew so well.

She saw Peggy and Percival before they were aware of her presence. Both of them were standing over one of the babies. Quietly, Louisa-Margaretta sighed. *How these strange little foundlings had changed everything at the home!* Sometimes, there was so much attention paid to the little bundles that it seemed the recovery of everyone who was mad was quite forgot. Louisa-Margaretta, as the youngest child in her family, found it intolerable when people lost their senses over babies.

Peggy and Percival had done so, though. Peggy was stroking the cheek of the child, who was making strange gurgling noises, but she was looking at her husband.

"You brought her here for me?"

"I know you always wanted to be a mother, Peggy. And seeing how well you were with the other children, I thought this would be our chance to have a family."

A tear slid down Peggy's face. "But her family. We have taken her from them."

"She came from the foundling hospital. And when we find her family, they shall be invited to live with us."

Peggy stared at him, her features sharp. "It would cause such a scandal," she said. "Taking a baby from a foundling hospital but keeping a hearth warm for the babe's parents? I have never heard of such a thing."

"Have you heard of parents who do not miss their child every day of the separation? If I am to be her father, I know my heart will always be with her. My father does not often speak, but he has told me enough that I understand this."

Peggy nodded, touching Percival's arm. "Well, when are we to leave?"

The forest was glowing around them as the sun began to set, the sky turning pink as purple clouds swept across the horizon. "It will soon be dark," he said. "Perhaps as a family, we may remove to the village, if Joyce can recommend a nurse for the little one. That will give us more than enough time to plan for the future."

"Oh, Percival," she said. "What if I should fail again and end up here? Only, then you will have a daughter to care for."

"It is I who failed," he said and took out a handkerchief. "If I had only been honest from the first, your nerves would not have had to take so much. And I should have come with you in the carriage and slept at the very gates of this place. In the future, Peggy, I don't intend to be separated from either of you. They can kill me first."

"And the army?"

"No more. Where thou goest, I will go; and where thou lodgest, I will lodge."

Peggy smiled, her laughter ringing out. "It may be the Bible, darling, but you sound like a Quaker yourself."

And the two lost themselves in laugher, staring at the tiny mite's face.

**48**

———

The ladies were preparing for bed, but they were restless. Judith was called away from Mercy because Bathsheba was supposed to be caring for Anne, their new arrival. It appeared that Anne was in difficulties, and as Mercy was hardly likely to wake from her deep slumber, Judith did not feel too guilty leaving her in the care of the taciturn Clarinda.

Anne might well be taking Clarinda's place, Judith reflected, as the latter was so much recovered that she was entrusted with the care of others. But Judith felt that Anne ought not to have come. The home was not a fit place for anyone with a murderer on the loose. Anne, though she did not share in the secret, seemed to agree with this sentiment.

"I can't be here," she said, pacing about the room she was supposed to be sharing with Esther. "Oh, where is my baby?"

Judith entered the little room quietly and with great caution.

Bathsheba was sitting on the small room's only chair, staring at the wall.

Esther, who had been so distraught over the superintendent's death that she could not leave her bed, was trying to soothe Anne. "All will be well," she said, moving as if she meant to touch her then hesitating.

Anne flung her arms out wildly, knocking Esther into Judith.

"My child! Where is she?"

"Bathsheba, may I speak with thee?" Judith asked gently. "Esther, go fetch us some cloths, please."

Esther looked back over her shoulder as she left the room, as if she could not trust any of the three young ladies who remained.

Judith swallowed a sigh, beckoning to Bathsheba to follow her into the passageway. When the other woman was close enough, Judith kept her eyes on Anne as she and Bathsheba conversed.

"Bathsheba, did Anne lose a child?"

"No, but she and her child have been parted."

"Why?"

"Because she went mad," said Bathsheba, glaring. "She could not care for a baby in this state."

"I am sure she did not wish to be mad or to be parted from her child."

"Then she ought to have done more."

Sighing, Judith went back into the room. She had studied Margaret's conviction that nobody would choose madness until she believed it herself. When she started feeling that those about her were choosing to be "difficult" in their behavior, she always knew she needed to cure such thoughts with a rest.

But Bathsheba would have to keep working. They were all in danger. There would be no resting.

Judith took a tolerant but scolding voice with Anne, who

was still pacing and shouting. "Please keep thy voice quiet. We mustn't wake the baby."

Anne grew quieter in the involuntary harmony of a conversation.

"Where is my child?" Anne asked again but with curiosity and trust in her voice.

"The nurse will bring her," said Judith. "For the moment, help me fold some cloths, please."

Esther came in, her arms piled high with the embroidery from the workbasket. Though the quality of the designs and the stitching varied greatly, Anne did not appear to notice. Judith sat on the bed with her, and they went through the pile, folding each one.

"Where is my baby?" Anne asked again. "I don't like to be parted from her."

"Of course not," said Judith. "You'll see her very soon."

The story she was creating for Anne gave her an answer about the murder, and she looked up sharply when Louisa-Margaretta knocked on her door.

## 49

Judith hardly slept, and she knew Louisa-Margaretta must have been the same. They waited until the next morning to speak to Margaret and Bathsheba, as it was exceedingly difficult for four ladies to be spared from their duties at the same time. Only on a Sunday morning, when many of them would be at their meeting, was it possible.

Joyce was with all the children, and she had fashioned a way to take them out for a walk with one of the ladies who had stayed behind. With the servants away, Judith, Louisa-Margaretta, Margaret, and Bathsheba were able to speak on the porch.

"Thank you for bringing us together," said Margaret. "But our time is short. What is your question?"

Louisa-Margaretta spoke first. "We know that your late husband killed the doctor. And we know why."

Bathsheba flinched, but Margaret did not move.

"What is it you imagine you know?" Margaret asked.

"You brought your daughter back, Bathsheba," said Louisa-Margaretta. "She was Mr Fortescue's child, and he would not leave the home, nor would he countenance the baby's removal. Your father discovered this late, and it came as a shock to him."

Both of the Lamb women were still silent, and Judith found herself nearly in tears at the strange situation.

"I do not understand why you could not have raised the child. Pretended she was a foundling then kept her with you as a ward. Or a cousin's babe or something of the sort."

"We could have," said Bathsheba. "But my father would have none of it. Said that he would not raise a child conceived out of wedlock and that he would not let me leave with her. Because I would have gone anywhere rather than be parted from her."

Her voice grew stronger as she spoke, and Margaret sent her a look that Judith struggled to interpret.

"Yes, well," Margaret said. "My husband and I quarreled. I will regret my actions until death and beg the Lord's forgiveness. Is that all the two of you had to tell us?"

Judith stared at the woman she had admired.

Louisa-Margaretta, who always found humour when she was in difficulties, laughed. "Certainly not. Surely you mean to turn yourself in. I'm sorry. Thou. Thou meanest to turn thyself in."

Margaret shook her head. "And leave everyone here to fend for him or herself in the wild, uncompromising world beyond our gates? That would not do, surely."

Judith still could not speak.

"Come, Judith. As it turns out, Margaret is madder than anyone who has ever come to the home."

They walked away in silence then turned and stopped.

Judith looked back at the porch. Margaret, ever the stronger of the pair, was comforting her daughter.

"She would do anything to protect her child," Judith said softly.

"Bathsheba? Yes, I suppose she would. That's why she killed her father."

Judith nodded. "I was speaking of Margaret, who is the same. She would protect Bathsheba with her last breath."

"Well, neither of them is ever going to admit to it. And they seem to believe the home ought to guarantee some protection. After all, it is already in danger and will certainly be shuttered if the truth ever emerges."

Judith's stomach lurched. "So we are to keep such a secret in the name of protecting the mad?"

Either path seemed equally impassable to her. She couldn't deprive people like Peggy of the one place where they could become well again, but she also could not condone murder.

"I suppose we have no choice," said Louisa-Margaretta. "Though what I am to tell Mr Fortescue, I am sure I cannot say."

Judith started. "Your promise to him!"

"Never mind. On the subject of persistent men, there is one waiting for you under the tree not a hundred yards away. Do go to him, and may you fare better than I have."

"Louisa-Margaretta," said Judith, who would rather speak to her friend than the man who still made her heart soar and fall fitfully.

"Go. Mr Fortescue is to call on me shortly. I shall think of something."

# 50

Judith did not feel surprised to see Morgan waiting for her. She knew she ought to call him Mr Morgan Ramsbury still, and if there was any call to address him, she would do so. But every inch of his face was familiar, and when she saw him standing outside the garden, she began to feel the peace Louisa-Margaretta had once described. After all, she loved only him, and she would continue to love him just as well her whole life. There was not much point in dissembling. Judith knew in her bones that even if he left forever after hearing what she had to say, her love would remain just as strong. It was fitting, she thought, that he had sought shade underneath the only tree there, a green willow. She could not have spoken about his feelings, but hers were quite clear.

"I am ready to be a Quaker," she said, surprising even herself. "If that is what God asks of me, I've no objection."

The joy in his face was evident, but he hesitated. "Thou wished to tell me something else, did thee not?"

"Yes. Louisa-Margaretta and I have discovered the culprits. And we do not plan to name them."

She had understood her friend's decision before either of them was certain, and as she spoke the words, she knew she would stand by them.

"So if we are to remain friends," she said carefully, "you must be very certain that you can live with my decision."

"I am surprised by thee, Judith," he said gently, leaning slightly toward her. "Has not thou always held that a murderer must be found and punished? Yet it seems that now, when someone has taken the lives of two of the best men who have ever devoted themselves to such work, you are inclined to turn away."

"I have always held that it is not for me to judge. That is God's role. And I'm sure it is easy enough to see that when I have looked for murderers in the past, it was always to spare the living first."

"I do not suppose Louisa-Margaretta will tell me either," he said, looking down at the trunk of the tree. "She has always loved thee as a true friend, and she would see through it at once if I tried to dissemble."

Judith smiled at his observation and was touched that he had understood her friend. Louisa-Margaretta's sense of family honor might have kept her away from Judith for a great while, but Judith had only recently realised that Louisa-Margaretta's affection had not actually wanted. Though she could be thoughtless, she was certainly loyal, and Judith knew instinctively that they would mean a great deal to each other in years to come.

Just as Morgan would mean a great deal to her. And part of her heart told her to tell him so, to confess all her love beneath the thick and protective branches of the green willow, where none would see or hear.

But she fought it. If he could not help but consider her complicit in the murderers, she was not likely to see him again, and it would not be right to burden him with such knowledge. Also, her heart still held whispers of pride and fear. She was not a young woman who complained if she had a stone in her shoe or if her throat tickled her and she wanted to cough during one of her father's sermons. When she had spent a lifetime without confessing even small disappointments and minor points of discomfort, it would take a great deal to turn her into someone who went about using flowery words to talk about the state of her heart.

"Yes?" he asked, and the way he looked at her made her think he might have discerned her thoughts anyway.

"I have said as much as I can. And now you only have to decide whether we might stay friends or you cannot accept this decision."

"That is simple," he said firmly. "Of course we shall always remain friends. As to the silence itself, I must think on it. After all, these men were friends to me and to all of the poor souls who have sought refuge here, and I—well, as I said, I may not ever become reconciled with losing them in this manner."

*They were* not *friends to all who sought refuge here,* thought Judith. The doctor had been no great friend to her, and the superintendent had tried to reject all three of the foundlings. One could hardly imagine a more vulnerable being seeking refuge. Even William on his worst day was more capable than an infant. But Morgan did not know any of that, and though it broke her heart not to share it with him, she could not change that part of her decision.

The leaves of the tree rustled, and he stepped closer to her. "Miss St Clair," he said slowly. "Would it be terribly imprudent if I asked to kiss you?"

Morgan had always been a respectful suitor, concerned for Judith's reputation, but when they were not observed, he was revealed to be not quite what a chaperone would have wished. After all, he was a man who desired her, and they quickly learned to appreciate both the solitude and the privacy that the willow tree provided.

He cleared his throat, stepping back from her. "It is not right," he said. "It is not fair to thee, and I must apologise for myself again."

Judith could not speak. She wished he would not apologise, that he would forgive her and kiss her again in the same breath, but he only touched his hat.

"Please give my best wishes to my cousin and to all your family," he said hastily, and she had to part the leaves of the willow in order to watch him as he walked away.

Then she had to close the leaves around her again, for she was crying.

# 51

The parlour was silent. Margaret and Bathsheba must have gone off to find the children, since there was no reason for them to pretend they were not interested.

Mr Fortescue was sitting in his chair, leaning back as if he were in his own home.

"So, little Miss Haddington," he said. "You tried, but you could not find a murderer. Well, no matter. Neither could I, and I despair of it now."

Louisa-Margaretta could admit failure when she and Judith had succeeded, but she had no intention of marrying Mr Fortescue. "I did not think you would allow your brother's death to go unavenged. It seems very much as though you are giving up."

"Moving forward, more like. For we are to be married."

"We are not," she said too quickly. "I should never have made such a promise."

"And now having failed, you intend to break it?"

"I do not intend to keep it."

"Ah," he said with a cold expression.

His features were still fine, but there was a cast of cruelty over them she had not noticed in their prior meetings. He looked quite capable of abandoning a woman such as Mercy.

"Well, my intentions lie elsewhere. The ladies of the haut ton bore me, as do their less salubrious equivalents in the street. You are the only interesting woman, Miss Haddington, and I intend to have you."

She stared at him, but he would not yield. She had learned to fence at one time, as her brother Sherborne had been interested in that pursuit for a season. And one of the things she remembered was that common strength would not be sufficient in the face of a formidable enemy. It was rather like chess, a game that had never interested Louisa-Margaretta but seemed to fascinate Judith. One must make a concession in order to best a stronger enemy.

"If in five years, I have not married, I will marry you."

His face grew stormy. "Yet you promised to marry me if you did not find this murderer, and you will be made to keep your word."

"I made no promise as to when I would marry you," said Louisa-Margaretta loftily. "Unless I marry within these five years, then I shall be keeping my word."

"And if you were to marry?"

"I suppose my future husband would have to challenge you, then."

When he began to laugh, she glared. "Or I would."

She did not need to tell him she was an excellent shot. It irritated her that, instead of looking scared, he seemed entranced once again.

"One year," he said. "You have until the end of next year, as I am a generous gentleman. Our engagement shall last nearly eighteen months."

Louisa-Margaretta tried to hide her triumph. She had been hoping only for a season or two, and eighteen months was much more time than she would have dared to demand.

"Very well." She stood to leave. "Good day, Mr Fortescue."

Surprise was written in his features, and he moved to grab her as she slipped out the door. But she had anticipated him, and she was too quick. As she walked across the lawn, all the people who had gone to the meeting were returning.

If she went back to work, he would not be able to follow her.

## 52

Judith and Louisa-Margaretta were side by side in the kitchen garden. For once, there were few dissenting voices. The day was beautiful, and the news that they would no longer be visited by the magistrate was most welcome. Apparently, the foolish gentleman had believed that both the doctor and the superintendent had died either naturally or at their own hands. And if there were suspicions of suicide, he would naturally be inclined to consider that they were not in their right minds. Indeed, the persistent kindness and piety of the Quakers combined with the strange nature of the home had so exhausted the man that he seemed determined to never come again. Judith had never even seen him. He seemed to avoid speaking to any of the women.

Louisa-Margaretta alone was unaffected by the halcyon days that seemed to pass by them like clouds in the untroubled sky. Her face was tight and grieved as she told Judith of Mr Fortescue's threats.

"You have over a year to consider his offer? But surely you could never even think of accepting."

"I must hope he finds a lady he likes more within the year, then," said Louisa-Margaretta bitterly. "Unless we are to choose someone from this place and give him a false name for a murderer."

Judith said nothing. *How easy that would have been to say to Morgan!* But she could not force herself to lie in that way, and she knew he would have seen through her if she attempted to dissemble.

Before she could find words to say to her friend, Mercy came up to her.

"What's happened, Mercy?"

Though Mercy was now well enough to stay with the other women, and the room that had been only for her and Judith had been abandoned, she still grieved for the husband she had once known well. And she was putting her hand to her head as if she were very tired or hot.

Mercy, swaying a bit, took some faded writing paper from her pocket. She'd gone through many different pieces of paper, and Judith had to write words that were clear and small.

Mercy pointed to the word *hungry* and looked up at Judith, blinking.

"We are about to eat," said Judith.

Mercy pointed to the words *I would like* on the front of the page then turned it over. On the back, Judith had written out the alphabet. She said the letters as Mercy pointed at them. "*R-E-T*. . . no, that was *S*? *P-I-T-E*."

Judith realised the ladies had all begun to laugh at her. Though she already understood, Mercy then turned the page over and pointed to the phrases *I would like* and *Finished with* while grinning at Judith.

"Thou wouldst like to be finished." Judith laughed. "I

understand, Mercy. Thou hast made thy sentiments very clear."

Louisa-Margaretta had smiled, but she was not laughing. It grieved Judith to see her friend so troubled.

"We shall rest from our labour, then," said Judith to the assembled ladies, and with some great merriment, they began to put away the tools.

Judith drew Louisa-Margaretta into the corner.

"Louisa-Margaretta, go back to Wycliffe Castle with me. We shall think of something—I promise—and at least we can be out of Mr Fortescue's reach in the coming months."

Louisa-Margaretta sighed. "Think of something? As in find a way for me to tolerate such a husband?"

"No," said Judith firmly, crossing her arms. "You will never marry him. But we must have a strategy for this battle. Of that, I am quite certain."

"I thought nursing madwomen was your vocation. You do not wish to give it up, surely? Unless you are running from my cousin?"

Judith coloured slightly. "Your cousin will decide for himself whether he can abide what we have done. No, I would go because living here is no way to hide from my family."

"Miriam is furious with you. You would brave her displeasure?"

"I shall have to brave it someday, and I daresay the home has fortified me."

The rest of the ladies went in for their meal, but Mercy circled back. She took Judith's arm, leading her into the large and strange building she would soon be leaving. And Louisa-Margaretta, after looking over her shoulder into the garden, followed them. For another evening, the home would be their sanctuary.

# ALSO BY EVE TARRINGTON

Two Spinsters and a Corpse

Two Spinsters and a Duel

Two Spinsters and a Thief

Two Spinsters and an Assassin

# ABOUT THE AUTHOR

Eve Tarrington is a Jane Austen fanatic. She has written dozens of books, but this is her first historical mystery set in the Regency era. She is thankful to her readers, her family, and her friends.

Would you like to know when Eve Tarrington is putting out a new novel? You're in luck! Join the mailing list at tena ciousteacuppress.com/eveTnews. You'll get an email when a new book is coming out.

In addition, you'll get a special copy of *Two Ladies and a Manhunt*, a subscriber bonus that follows young Judith and Louisa-Margaretta as they separately search for a young lady. When Louisa-Margaretta's friend disappears from one of the most exclusive London ballrooms shortly after coming out, suspicions and false accusations fly. For very different reasons, Judith and Louisa-Margaretta, still strangers, are intent on finding her killer.

# TWO LADIES AND A MANHUNT

Join the mailing list at tenaciousteacuppress.com/eveTnews to read the entire novella! In the meantime, please enjoy this introduction to *Two Ladies and a Manhunt*.

**1**

———

Louisa-Margaretta Haddington stood perfectly still, listening to a torrent of endearments and praise.

"Your beauty, Miss Haddington, can be compared only to the absolute perfection of your mind. You are the epitome of culture and grace, and I should not consider myself the least bit worthy of asking for your hand in marriage, were it not for one thing."

She could hear no more. "Really, I hardly think—"

"Hear me out. No man on earth could possibly be worthy of you, and since you must marry, I may as well ask. Why not choose me? For I certainly have several things to recommend me, though I would not propose to think myself your equal. For you are ever so divine—"

"Stop." Though she tried to look cross, she could not keep herself from laughing. "I am sure you are very wrong."

Louisa-Margaretta was tall, and though the praise for her beauty may have been exaggerated, it was still not far from the truth. Her tresses were reddish gold, her complexion radiant, her eyes lively. Her figure spoke to both perfect health and regular exercise, and all that was helped along by a surfeit of confidence. If Louisa-Margaretta had doubts, they were never about her own worth but only that of others.

Her friend Miss Lavinia Finch had been lying on the sofa, but she sat up and took a sip of tea. Though she had also been laughing as she professed her undying love for Louisa-Margaretta, she began to frown. After taking another lump of sugar, she stirred it into her tea. "Mr Fudge is far from stupid, in spite of his unfortunate name," she said. "You would be a fool not to consider his proposal."

Abandoning her tea, Louisa-Margaretta walked over to the pianoforte and began to play an etude. Though her technique was imperfect, she made up for it in the vivacity of her performance. "There has been no proposal," she said. "It would be improper before I am out."

Lavinia raised her eyebrows at her friend. "After tomorrow, you *will* be out."

Louisa-Margaretta sighed. "Yes, we shall both be out, I suppose. And I would rather die than be the next Mrs Fudge."

Glaring, Lavinia replied, "I am sure you would not wish to die, Louisa-Margaretta. There are many worse things than marrying an honourable man such as Mr Fudge."

Louisa-Margaretta switched to an aria, though she did not sing it. In truth, it was hard for her to imagine something worse than marrying Mr Christmas Fudge. He was twenty years older than her, not at all handsome, and a dear friend of both her parents. *At eighteen, am I to be a stepmother to his three children?* She could not bear even entertaining such an idea.

"You marry him, then," she said. "If you are willing to be Mrs Fudge, I shall wish you joy."

Lavinia was still glaring. "He has not offered any attentions to me, nor is he like to." And with that, she walked out of the room without a single word of goodbye.

"Did Lavinia leave so soon?" Louisa-Margaretta's mother asked, walking in and frowning at the tea things. "I wished to speak with her about tomorrow."

"Yes." Louisa-Margaretta had been answering Mama with only one word for days, and she was not going to give her any more information.

"Louisa-Margaretta." Mrs Haddington sat down next to her daughter. "I am sure that you may feel rather vexed, but ruining the reputation of our family is not the balm you are seeking. You must be polite to our callers, and tomorrow, you must put on your best smile at court. One does not snub the queen."

"Yes," said Louisa-Margaretta again. In truth, she had no quarrel with the queen, and she would not have any trouble with Mr Fudge if he did not insist on admiring her.

"Darling, if you will not listen to me, look to God for guidance."

"Yes," said Louisa-Margaretta again before escaping.

**2**

---

"These things are sent to try us," murmured Judith St Clair to her cousin Dorothy St Clair.

"It is not trying," said Dorothy. "Never, because I am not going to be defeated! I shall not accept it, Judith."

Tears of anger were streaking down her face. Judith, who was used to comforting people who grieved, found herself perplexed.

Of course, Judith's younger sister, Miriam, often cried over life's smaller trials. But ever since they had arrived in London for a visit, little Miriam had spent much of her time with their young cousin Rollo. At eleven, Miriam liked ribbons, but she was not interested in the talk of balls and coming out. She would rather run about with Dorothy's youngest brother, enjoying the sights of the city street from the window and getting paint on her best frock during their artistic endeavours.

"I am sure there are partners aplenty to be found outside of Almack's." Judith hated dancing and felt relieved that the most prestigious location in London was very far out of her reach.

"Not the sort of partner I would wish to marry," said Dorothy, sobbing again.

Judith tried a little pat on the shoulder then murmured some words of comfort before abandoning her cousin. If she kept trying to soothe her companion, she would likely say something that revealed her complete indifference.

When Judith sought solitude in her parents' room, her mother tried to rise from the bed. "I am sorry, dear," she said. "I should have been the one to comfort Dorothy."

"Her mother should do it." Judith knew she should not grumble, but as she took her mother's hand, she felt both more petulant and more comfortable.

"One of us should," said Mrs St Clair. "But as none of us had any expectations from Almack's, it is hard to know exactly what to tell her."

Judith's mother had carried at least three children since Miriam's birth but given birth to none. She had passed the time when things seemed to go wrong. Still, Judith was anxious and chastised herself for upsetting her mother.

"What is it, dear?" asked her mama gently. "You can tell me, you know. You and your father have been tiptoeing about for months. Only Miriam tells me things now."

Judith swallowed. She wished she could have told her father, but even with his gentle nature, she was quite sure he would not understand.

"I don't wish to be out," she said. "Oh, Mama, I feel the same as I did last year. Must I accompany Dorothy to balls?"

Mama sighed. "Yes. You are nineteen now, Judith. And your cousin is depending on you."

Judith turned away. She refused to argue more, but she

could not imagine throwing herself into the world that Dorothy seemed to take for granted. The harsh conversations about wealth, birth, and childbearing prospects that she had heard her whole life seemed entirely apart from what she wished. It all seemed so very unholy. *How can my parents, who raised me to love and respect God and my fellow man, go in for such a thing?*

"Mama," she said.

But her mother shook her head. "You must be kind to Dorothy. She's had a very trying year, watching all her brothers and sisters leave."

Judith left the room. Of course Dorothy had been going through a trying time, but it didn't follow that Judith must be thrown into a marriage market so merciless that it was sure to make her own year equally trying. At least, she hoped not.

**3**

"Lou, you must be kind to Christmas, now," said her father. "He's had a trying year."

The Haddingtons were all gathered in their sitting room, as they had gotten word that Mr Fudge was going to call. Mr and Mrs Haddington as well as their son Sherborne were happily anticipating the visit.

"I have had a trying year myself," said Louisa-Margaretta. Perhaps it was not fair, but she found herself being gentle with her father, though he had the same annoying demands as Mama. "Why is there no sympathy for the sort of year I have had? Dragged to London for the season, deprived of my horses, forced to parade about in all sorts of silly clothing."

Papa only laughed. "Very silly," he agreed, chortling. "The hoops!"

Louisa-Margaretta saw her opening. Her father agreed that the ceremony of being presented at court was ridiculous. Perhaps she could enlist him, and they could talk Mama out of that particular requirement.

Mr Fudge's voice put the idea out of her mind. He had

entered the room and was greeting everyone warmly. She had to stop herself from sticking her tongue out at him. For years, they had gotten on well, as her fondness for the hunt and for her brother's constant games of cricket had amused him. Now she could hardly bring herself to look at him.

"It is wonderful to see you, Christmas," said Mama. "I trust we may see a great deal of each other now that we are back in London." Their country house was not twenty miles outside the city, but Mama always talked about it as if it were worlds away.

"I very much hope so," he said. His voice was low and gentle. Mr Fudge was one of the few people whose manners never seemed to change or slip. He was always polite, never condescending.

"I was hoping to see you all at Almack's... perhaps the day after tomorrow?" Though he addressed the group, it was plain that Lousia-Margaretta's company was his greatest interest.

Louisa-Margaretta's father grinned. "No. I'm afraid not."

Mr Fudge drew in a breath, and for a moment, the attention was away from Louisa-Margaretta.

"Not again," said Mr Fudge mildly.

"Yes!" answered Papa, sounding delighted. "Every year, in fact."

Sherbourne, who hated dancing and avoided Almack's as a rule, looked extremely confused. "What is every year?"

"They don't let Papa go," said Louisa-Margaretta. "It's a way of punishing Mama for not marrying where those harpies thought she should."

"Louisa-Margaretta. Honestly, you know your father would rather not attend. And I, myself, would prefer to be in church. But because it is your season—"

"Keep Papa out?" asked Sherborne. Of all the

Haddington children, he looked most like his father. But his brown hair was thicker, his dark eyes more arrogant. He had always wanted to be his father's partner in business but much preferred London to Manchester. Though he liked to think he was just as practical as his father, who had grown up poor, he was a product of his comfortable upbringing.

Mr Fudge shook his head. "It really is unconscionable, the way they split up families. If you would like me to have a word?"

"They wouldn't listen to even a magistrate, my dear," said Mama. "And truly, we need to stay in favour for our Louisa-Margaretta's sake. Otherwise, I would consider having a word myself."

"Harpies," said Sherbourne, which earned him a hard look from both his parents. "What? I'm sure they don't even know everyone by sight. If I were to go with one of my poorest friends from Oxford but dress him up in expensive clothing and claim he was a cousin, I am quite sure they would admit us."

"The day after tomorrow sounds delightful," said Mama pointedly. "Sherbourne, I am sure you will join us in your father's place. As I mentioned, it is important for your sister."

Sherbourne looked mutinous, and Louisa-Margaretta was secretly delighted that two of her parents' children were cross with them at once. Augustus was the only other Haddington staying at the London home, but he was to be married in two weeks and spent many hours with his bride.

"I can't think of a worse place in London," he said. "Nothing good to eat or drink and the worst possible company." After a pause, he added, "Meaning no offence, I'm sure, Mr Fudge."

"None taken," said their visitor, sitting and smiling at them all.

Louisa-Margaretta tried to keep herself from groaning. She could hardly tell which thing she dreaded more, being presented at court or being forced into an evening of dancing with Mr Fudge.

**4**

———

Louisa-Margaretta and Lavinia shared a carriage. It had been arranged beforehand that their mothers would arrive separately, as the costumes the girls were wearing were so large as to make sharing the confined space impossible for more than two young ladies. And though Louisa-Margaretta had better friends, she had always gotten on well with Lavinia until the day before.

She was not one to apologise, but Lavinia did not share that characteristic.

"Louisa-Margaretta," she said, "I'm sorry I was cross with you yesterday."

Their carriage was admitted to the grounds of the palace, perhaps at the very moment when even the most confident young lady might start to feel some nerves at the idea of being in Queen Charlotte's presence.

"You still seem rather cross," said Louisa-Margaretta, not looking at her friend.

"Yes, well, these circumstances would be trying for a better woman," said Lavinia, a pained look on her face.

Louisa-Margaretta examined her own costume and sighed. The hoops were large, the fabric distinctly uncomfortable. White crepe with a good deal of lace and ornamentation, it was the sort of garment that begged for a stain. She wondered when she was going to be able to eat another meal.

"These hoops shouldn't be so large," she murmured, trying to push hers into a better shape. "I feel ridiculous."

"We're fortunate they are," said Lavinia darkly. "We can all look equally ridiculous. Lord, what a silly show."

"Are you not happy to be seeing Queen Charlotte?" asked Louisa-Margaretta. Though she was dreading the spectacle, she would have thought her old friend might enjoy such a thing. Lavinia had always spoken of any brushes with royalty with great reverence.

"Perhaps I would be," she said tonelessly. "Tell me... What would you think if you knew this were the last time you would ever see this palace?"

Louisa-Margaretta had been distracted, thinking of how much time she would have to spend in the dull charade before she could beg her mother to leave, and the question sounded odd to her. "Lavinia, what do you mean?"

But the moment had passed. Lavinia was gazing out at the palace walls, waiting for the carriage to stop so she could step out. "Forget what I said. It is of no consequence."

Louisa-Margaretta frowned. "I wish you would tell me."

She would forget that conversation after, in the bustle of the presentation and her curiosity about the other men and women who were presented to Queen Charlotte. She had heard a rumour that the king was unwell, but they all had a chance to see him. And he did not look terribly indisposed as he cut a cake that was fully six feet tall, to the gasped admiration of the crowd.

She ought to have asked Lavinia what she meant. Later, she would have great cause to regret not doing so.

**5**

———

Louisa-Margaretta had begged her mother to take her shopping. If she were to go dancing, at least she could wear the worst dress she could possibly find —something that would send a message to a suitor like Mr Fudge and would put him off her forever. At Queen Charlotte's ball the day before, he had hoped to dance with her, but she had retreated to a different room with what she claimed were nerves. Her mother had not been fooled, but unwilling to make a scene, Mrs Haddington had accepted the excuse. In the morning, she chastised her daughter, letting her know plainly that they would never go back to the country unless Louisa-Margaretta made an effort in London.

She could not have thought of any argument better suited to forcing her only daughter into compliance. Louisa-Margaretta, determined to dance, joined her mother in a dressmaker's shop while her father and brother went to call on an acquaintance.

"I think that black would suit me," Louisa-Margaretta said. "Something like this."

The garment she had found was a worsted day dress made in a very deep grey. It might have done well for a widow, but she would be laughed out of a ballroom.

Mama was not fooled for an instant. "You are not wearing such a thing to Almack's. I don't know why we came. Look, there are Papa and Sherbourne waiting in the carriage. If this is what you had in mind for a purchase, we may as well go join them."

They left the shop empty-handed. Papa stepped out of the carriage and handed up his wife then followed Louisa-Margaretta back in after helping her up.

"I'm not sure why I must be forced to wear something in a gay colour," said Louisa-Margaretta as her mother began murmuring something to Papa about the horrid ball they were supposed to hold in her honour.

"White is a symbol of death in many countries," said Sherborne. "You could go in white muslin in a funereal sense."

Louisa-Margaretta pouted. "I shall be forced to go in white muslin," she said. "But I won't do any dancing."

A family passed their carriage. It consisted of a handsome woman, the roundness of her belly not quite perfectly concealed under a light gown and a coat, a pretty young daughter, and a plainer, dark-haired daughter about Louisa-Margaretta's age. Louisa-Margaretta smiled. So sour did the older daughter look as she was steered into the shop by her mother. They looked too poor to have to worry about Almack's, but the pressure for a good marriage was nearly universal for young women. As was the resistance to it, apparently.

Louisa-Margaretta looked over to see her father holding his head in his hands, her mother looking grim.

"Papa!" she said, shocked. Her father, as a rule, did not believe in illness.

"It's nothing," he managed, looking at her. "A headache."

"Anyone could get a headache from waiting in front of shops all day," said Sherborne. "Let's go home. We must all be fresh for the evening."

Though he had meant to tell a joke, Louisa-Margaretta could not help but agree.

JOIN the mailing list at tenaciousteacuppress.com/eveTnews to get the entire novella and finish the story!